THE LIST OF JOHNNY'S VICTIMS READ LIKE THE TOWN'S SOCIAL REGISTER

Among them were all the "best" people in town, including:

FRANK HUBERT, civic leader, whose past was a matter of record — on many a police blotter.

KITTY MOCKRIDGE, wife of a rising young executive, who had married the man of her dreams without telling him about her nightmare past.

MERRILL KETCHUM, big businessman, who had clawed his way to the top by using any shortcuts he could find, legal or illegal.

Now that Johnny was dead, they should have been safe. But there was that whispering voice on the telephone that warned them their troubles had only begun . . . .

HERE'S WHAT THE CRITICS SAID:

The Sound of Insects

Mildred Davis

author of:
The Voice on the Telephone

MANOR
BOOKS
INC.

To Kathy

A MANOR BOOK

First printing ....April, 1967
Second printing .... April, 1974

Manor Books Inc.
329 Fifth Avenue
New York, New York 10016

Library of Congress Catalog Card Number: 66-12239

The Sound

of Insects

I

A cicada gave an anguished screech just as Stacy stepped out on the terrace for air. Looking down, she saw a large black and yellow wasp beside the cicada it had just stabbed and paralyzed. The wasp turned its victim on its back and dragged it, head foremost and feet in the air, along the tangled grass and clover.

As though she herself were the helpless prey of a gigantic monstrosity, she watched the wasp and its quarry disappear into the dark burrow. At that moment her mind took over for her eyes and she followed the two of them to their underground destination. In the inch-wide chamber two feet under the earth, the wasp egg would be attached to the cicada's body, and there the latter would have to await its fate: a three-day vigil in darkness and terror, and finally the emergence of the wormy, ravenous larva. Then would begin the feast on the living body.

"You look as though you'd just seen a ghost, Miss Hubert."

Stacy blinked, brushed back the loose, swinging hair, and turned to see who had spoken. It was a man she didn't know, but more than that, it was a man whom she felt didn't belong to Highlands—her Highlands, that is. He was certainly dressed nicely, and his speech was no worse than Merrill Ketchum's, and his complexion was no darker than Gibson Newhouse's, but he was absolutely non-Highlands.

"Oh—it's silly of me. I just saw . . . well, I'd better explain. I teach biology—"

"You *teach?*" His voice couldn't have expressed more incredulity than if she had said she sold narcotics to teenagers.

"Why, yes. I—"

"You look as though you're still in high school."

"Well, thank you—I think."

"Where do you teach?"

"Highlands Country Day."

"Oh." He nodded to himself as though that confirmed something he was thinking.

"Have you tasted those little hot things with the crunchy fillings? They're absolutely divine."

"Tell me something, Miss Hubert. Why do girls like you always use words like divine?"

The blood rushed to Stacy's face. She was tall but slight, and her blond hair hung straight past her shoulders. That, combined with a soft, baby face, made people take her for five or six years younger than her twenty-four. It also deceived them about her intelligence.

Tell me something, Mr. Whatever-your-name-is, she answered silently, why do men like you always try to attract the attention of girls like me by being outrageous? But she didn't say it aloud, and therein, she decided, lay the difference between Highlands and non-Highlands. Aloud, she said, "It *is* a silly word. But then, most of us *do* use a daily vocabulary of about two hundred words. Let's go in, Mr. uh—"

"Ritacco. Joseph Ritacco. I'm Johnny MacLeod's weekend guest."

"Yes. Of course." She took his arm and led him in.

The French doors had all been left open to allow a free flow of

8

guests from the terraces to the downstairs rooms. Angela Hubert's mums and zinnias packed every available vase, and the house, generally subdued-looking in golds and whites, was hectically colorful. The caterer's helpers threaded in and out with trays of champagne and canapés.

Looking for a likely candidate on whom to foist Mr. Ritacco, Stacy passed up two women ("She won't go to any party Marge goes to. You know how Marge and Carl have been carrying on."), three men and a woman ("—played a third-round seventy-one, and don't forget it's one of the most difficult courses on which the Open was played.") in favor of her father ("Everybody's for freedom, just like everybody is against sin. But what do they mean by freedom?")

Waiting for an opening, she said, "Excuse me, Dad. This is Mr. Ritacco—"

Beside her, Ritacco said, "Really, Stacy—I hope you don't mind me calling you Stacy—I don't need looking after. Now stop being a good little hostess and relax." But to Stacy's relief, her father turned to her. Automatically he put his left hand around her shoulders and held out his right. "Mr. Ritacco? Glad to meet you. Dr. Trowbridge—he's our minister so don't tell him your physical problems—Mr. Ritacco."

Ritacco hesitated a moment, and Stacy, surprised, glanced at him. Then belatedly his hand came out but he was frowning. "Hubert? Haven't we met before?"

"I don't believe so."

"I'm a newspaperman—I tend to remember faces. Were you ever in Chicago?"

The hand resting on Stacy's shoulder twitched, but Frank Hubert's face remained bland and smiling. Uneasily Stacy smoothed down her white cotton dress, wondering what was happening.

"Chicago? Never. So you're a newspaperman. Let me introduce you to John Gaillord. He publishes—"

9

Stacy moved out of earshot and helped herself to champagne. She looked around for Will, but he was talking to two women, so she settled for her friend Kitty Mockridge.

"Stacy, you don't look like a girl who's announcing her engagement."

"I don't? Well, I suppose it's because I just saw this wasp dragging off this cicada to eat it—"

"Darling—all over the world, insects are eating one another. Why, in some places, even men—"

"—and it doesn't seem right for me to be enjoying myself while he's being digested. Or maybe I'm having second thoughts. Isn't the bride-to-be supposed to get cold feet just about now?"

"No, only the groom. But if you've changed your mind, let's tell Will. If he shops quickly, he may get another girl before your father makes the announcement."

"Don't tell me you're sick of Healey already."

"*Me?* I wasn't thinking of me. I like them big and burly. Not skinny with nothing to hug."

They weaved in and out until they found Will Tobin and waited for him to finish what he was saying to a pretty, middle-aged woman ("Treat them right and they'll eat the way you do, talk the way you do, keep their houses clean the way you do—").

"*My* house is dirty," volunteered Kitty.

Not hearing her, the woman said in a soft, Southern drawl, "You're wrong, Will. I know them better than you do. But an engagement party is no place for a discussion of this sort."

She kissed Stacy and wandered off. When she was out of earshot, Kitty said tipsily, "They *do* talk the way she does."

"Will," Stacy told her fiancé, "Kitty says you're too skinny for hugging."

"Some people care only for quantity."

Frank Hubert rapped for attention, and gradually the noise

10

diminished. While he made his short announcement speech, people smiled at Stacy and Will. Because the room was warm, a pink tint overlaid her tan, giving her skin the luminescence of a pearl. She was the perfect bride to be—pretty but not startlingly so, self-confident, but not obnoxiously so, at home with herself and the world. She clung to Will as though drawing nourishment from an invisible cord, and he smiled at her, half sardonically, half protectively. "And they say the Samoans have odd mating customs," he muttered.

When the speech was over, the ladies kissed Stacy and the men congratulated Will with more fervor than formality. Only two people didn't join the general activity, Joseph Ritacco, who didn't know anyone, and a boy of about Stacy's age who leaned against the farthest wall and watched her miserably. He was large and athletic-looking, but still boyish—unformed without being weak. He tried earnestly not to glance in Stacy's direction, but his eyes were continuously drawn that way as if a puppeteer were manipulating them. He kept taking large gulps of Scotch.

Stacy was completely unaware of him. As the guests broke into groups again, she heard someone say, "Jim Hostetter! I can't believe it!" She turned to see who it was.

Elena Ketchum, Stacy's mother's closest friend, was saying, "What reason could he have?"

"For what, Aunt Elena?"

"Oh Stacy—I didn't know you were there. Not today—"

Feeling slightly uneasy, Stacy said, "Sherry Hostetter was one of my students last year. What about Mr. Hostetter?"

The woman with Elena said bluntly, "Jim Hostetter committed suicide this afternoon."

Stacy put down her glass carefully. She hardly knew Mr. Hostetter, but a sudden chill made her hand unsteady. Rubbing her upper arms, she wondered what was wrong with her. It had all started with that ridiculous wasp—what a silly thought.

"Two children—a lovely wife—what in the world made him do a thing like that?"

"Did he leave a note?"

"I just this minute heard about it. I don't know any of the details."

"He always seemed so normal."

Unexpectedly Kitty said, "It's not necessarily abnormal to kill oneself."

"Why of course it's abnormal," Elena Ketchum rebuked her gently. "At the very least it's temporary insanity."

"That depends upon the society, doesn't it? I mean, well in Japan, for instance, at least in prewar Japan, if a man lost face, it was abnormal to continue living."

"Who lost face? What's going on?" Teetering unsteadily, Johnny MacLeod had come up quietly behind Kitty. She turned so quickly, she spilled her drink. She bent down to rub the spot on the carpet with her napkin, and Stacy could see that her piquant features had sharpened. Stacy had witnessed Kitty's reaction to Johnny MacLeod many times before, and each time it had surprised her. As far as Stacy was concerned, he seemed to be a completely innocuous kind of person who couldn't inspire a strong emotion in anyone. He was older than the two girls and had never married, because, some people said, he had to support a widowed mother, and others, less charitable, hinted he was also supporting a friend, a male friend. He came from a family which was "good," but not as good as it had been, and as a youngster had always been in trouble, but the kind of trouble tolerated by Highlands—drunken bouts, car accidents, mild property destruction on Hallowe'en. He had been graduated from a second-class college and occupied a second-class position in a first-class company. There was apparently no reason for Kitty's odd behavior.

"I have to wash this sticky mess off my hands," Kitty said. "Excuse me, all."

On impulse Stacy followed her upstairs. She supplied her with a comb and lipstick, and repaired her own makeup. From time to time she glanced at Kitty's pale face. "How about a bicarb?" she asked finally.

"No, I'm fine. Anyway, there's no remedy for Johnny Mac-Leod. Who's that man he brought here?"

"Mr. Ritacco? A newspaperman."

"How does Johnny know him?"

"I think Mrs. MacLeod said something about his doing a story about that whatchmecallit—electronic componetry for computers?—so, of course, he went to Narco—"

"Why go to Johnny? Why not Healey or even Merrill Ketchum?"

"Lowly newspaper reporters don't start with Merrill Ketchum—or even Healey, if you don't mind my saying so. They start with little assistant department heads of advertising and publications—"

"God, he turns my stomach."

"Who? Mr. Ritacco?"

"Johnny MacLeod."

"That's like saying milk toast turns your stomach. There isn't enough substance in Johnny to turn a—a—there ought to be a clever little metaphor there somewhere."

Kitty looked at her a moment with absolutely no expression and then she said, "Where's my favorite teenager? I haven't seen her anywhere?"

"Probably in the kitchen, making a pig of herself. Let's look." Stacy never pressed a point, and the people who didn't know her well made the mistake of considering her indifferent. Kitty, who knew her well, squeezed her arm suddenly.

As Stacy had predicted, they found Caroline in the kitchen, sipping champagne and eating caviar, but also helping the Hubert maid, Gwen, fill a tray with glasses. Stacy's sister had been to the hairdresser's, and she wore a new blue shift, but

13

nevertheless she looked terrible. At fourteen she had all the ingredients of womanhood, but in the wrong proportions. Her feet were too large, her breasts too small, her pimples too prominent, her hands too noticeable, her hips too boyish and her personality too overwhelming.

"Who told you you could drink?" Stacy demanded. Unconsciously she became shrewish whenever she spoke to her sister.

Caroline rolled her eyes. "Are you kidding? It's your engagement party."

Gwen smiled at Kitty behind Stacy's back. "It's my fault. I told her she could."

"Kitty," Caroline said, stuffing hot meat on toast into her mouth, "did you see Andy Newhouse drowning his sorrow in drink? He'll probably kill himself when Stacy gets married."

"Where's *your* drink?" Stacy asked Gwen. Andy Newhouse's problems didn't interest her.

"I had some champagne," Gwen assured her.

"You ought to marry Andy, Stace," Caroline said casually. "He's nearer your age."

"And leave Will to you? But there's twenty years difference in *your* ages."

"Who said anything about marrying Will?" Caroline scowled and changed the subject. "Can I wear a long dress at the wedding?"

Kitty put an arm around Caroline's shoulders. "All bridesmaids wear long dresses. You'll look sensational."

"Stacy said I can't be a bridesmaid if I don't clear up my complexion."

"Heavens, am I glad *I* never had a big sister," Kitty said. "If you're not a bridesmaid, I won't be matron of honor."

Frank Hubert charged into the kitchen, looking for tomato juice, and stopped at the sight of the assemblage.

"What's going on?" He looked flushed and tired. "Maybe

14

we ought to move the party in here.''

"We're just leaving, Dad.''

"You too, Caroline.''

"Why me? There's nobody here my age.''

As they went out into the passageway, Kitty ducked into the library to join a small group there. "Stacy,'' her father said when they were alone, "what do you know about this man who came with Johnny MacLeod?''

"I think I'll have forms printed up.''

"What?''

"Nothing, Dad. It seems computers are the big thing today and his newspaper is doing a series of articles on them. Now, Johnny works for Narco Electronics—''

"Why didn't he go to Merrill Ketchum? Or Healey Mockridge? They both—''

"I think there's an echo in here. Merrill Ketchum is an executive vice-president—oh heck, I don't know. Maybe that's why Johnny brought him. To introduce him to Merrill—''

"Never mind. Did he—did he say how long he was a newspaperman?''

For the first time Stacy became aware of all the lines in her father's face. He had never seemed old before. "What's wrong, Dad?''

Instantly his eyes dropped. Lightly he said, "It just hit me. In a few months you'll move out and never live with us again.''

She took his arm. "It *is* a thought, isn't it? I've never lived in any house but this one.''

"God—I was just remembering—I spent the whole night remembering—I know it sounds corny, but it just doesn't seem possible. I was remembering when you were about three —you'd always pretend to read books and watch us from the corner of your eye—once you read, 'I can fly as good as her,' and your mother said, 'I can fly as well as she can,' and you

15

looked back at the book and said, 'It says as good as her.' ''

"Frank!" a woman said with mock asperity, "I thought you were getting me tomato juice."

"Liz! I knew there was something I forgot!"

Stacy went back to the drawing room and snatches of conversation engulfed her again. "If her husband has been playing around for eight years, why worry about it now?" . . . "Foxcroft has something no other school has. For one thing—"

"To the sweetest, the prettiest bride I've ever known—that is, since I was married myself." It was Merrill Ketchum and he was lifting his glass to her.

"I'll drink to that," Will said, joining them.

"Lucky devil," Merrill told him. "Almost as lucky as I was twenty-five years ago."

Will tried hard to keep his eyes off Elena, who had gone somewhat downhill, as far as looks were concerned. Reading his mind, Stacy took a quick sip of her drink and sputtered. She was beginning to feel giddy. When Merrill had gone off, she said, "Well, you don't know what *I'll* look like in twenty-five years."

Grinning, he said, "My father always told me to look at the girl's mother. It's the only way to be sure."

"So that's why you're marrying me." There was no doubt that Angela Hubert was one of the best-looking women in the room. Her face was a narrowed-down, more angular version of Stacy's, and she was slim and well groomed.

"Do I use the same yardstick?" she asked, smiling at Will's father's paunch and receding hairline.

He laughed, and the two of them stood facing one another, not touching, sipping their drinks and smiling into one another's eyes. The voices eddied around them, but Stacy heard nothing until the non-Highlands voice said, "No, I just can't place him. But I'm sure I've met him before."

16

It was Joseph Ritacco and he was speaking to Johnny Mac-Leod. Johnny's mother, Harriet MacLeod, was sitting on a couch nearby and listening to the conversation.

Stacy turned back to her fiancé, but she felt the touch again, the cold chill of something unspeakable.

II

"Going out again?" Harriet MacLeod asked Johnny Monday evening. She stood in the doorway of his bedroom, watching him.

"Yes, ma'am," he said, adjusting his tie in front of the mirror.

"Why not stay home just this once? I'll be at Janet's tomorrow night. You can go out then."

He raised an eyebrow at her. "What's up?"

Looking depressed, she sat down on the edge of his bed. "Nothing's up. You were gone all weekend and now you're going out again."

"Who was gone all weekend? I was at the Huberts' Saturday."

"Well—don't quibble. You left right afterwards. I don't know why you have to spend so many weekends in the city. We never get a chance to talk anymore. We used to be so close—"

"Oh, come off it, Mumsy. No hearts and flowers."

She opened her mouth to continue, but just then she caught

sight of his face in the mirror. It was bland, pleasant, and heavy with warning, the familiar warning it always held when she left the narrow area he had long since chalked out for her—mind your own business or I'll walk out.

She got up, sighed audibly enough for him to hear, and went out into the hall. For a moment she hesitated between lying on the bed like a martyr or enjoying herself. Enjoyment won out and she went downstairs to switch on the new color television set he had bought her. He was generous with his money if not with his time.

Johnny had a busy evening ahead. Once his mother was settled, he consulted his records, jotted down some notes and then carefully filed the originals in an unusual spot.

His first stop was at the Huberts. He hadn't bothered to call in advance, but simply took his chances. In his years of experience, he had found it worked better that way. However, he had to accept the hazards, and when he walked in (he always entered people's houses without knocking if the doors were unlocked), Gwen, who happened to be passing the hall at the moment, told him the Huberts were out.

"Oh hell—I was hoping . . . do you mind telling me where they are?"

Gwen *did* mind. A little stiffly, she told him that Mr. Hubert, who was chairman of the Highlands Community Chest drive, was at a down-county conference, and that Mrs. Hubert was at a meeting called to discuss plans for a pool for the town's children.

"Stacy home?" Johnny asked pleasantly.

"No, she's out," Gwen said, volunteering nothing.

"Oh. Could I speak to Caroline for a minute?"

"Caroline!"

"Yes—just to chat."

"Come in, Mr. MacLeod." She led him towards a small

sitting room, but he headed independently for the staircase. "Wait here, please, Mr. MacLeod," Gwen said without sharpness, but firmly.

"Good God—I've known Caroline since she was born. I'll just—"

"Please sit down, Mr. MacLeod. I think she's in the shower." Frowning faintly, Gwen waited until he ambled into the sitting room. Immediately he picked up a cigarette box to inspect it, and then he examined Angela's collection of pillboxes. "Where's Stacy, by the way?" he called, conscious that she was still watching him.

Pretending not to hear, Gwen went upstairs, turning once to see if he was following. She went straight into Caroline's room without knocking. Caroline, who had long since come out of the shower, was wearing a head full of curlers and wrinkled pajamas. She was shaving her legs.

"Why don't you fold that cover back when you sit on it?" Gwen asked automatically. She had said the same thing daily for four years.

"Oh—I forgot. Besides, the blanket's itchy."

"Mr. MacLeod is here. He wanted to talk to someone else, but since no one else was here, he said he'd see you."

"*Mr*. MacLeod—oh, you mean Johnny. What does *he* want?"

"He didn't tell me."

"Oh heck. These curlers." Grumbling, she found a cotton robe with several buttons missing and put it on. Everything she owned seemed well born, but once in her hands, on the way downhill.

Not bothering to take out the curlers, and walking barefoot (everything about her pointing up her opinion of Johnny Mac-Leod), she went out on the landing and down the stairs.

Johnny was examining an enameled pillbox when she entered the room, but with exaggerated politeness he jumped to his feet and held a chair for her. "That's a snappy getup," he commented. His voice was a little odd. He tried to make it sound like an older man being kind to a child, but it emerged with a touch of licentiousness.

"I wasn't expecting company," Caroline said indifferently. She had no awareness of the licentiousness.

He laughed uproariously as though she had been terribly witty. "Next time I drop by I'll send in my coachman with my card."

Not knowing what was expected of her and feeling uncomfortable, she said nothing. Instead she turned on a small radio, searching for music. Finally she found what she wanted—a tone-deaf, nasal teenager moaning about his high school sweetheart.

"How's Buzzy?"

This time she turned a violent red, but at the same time she looked pleased. "How do *you* know about Buzzy?" she asked offhandedly.

"Oh—I get around. When will your mother and father be home?" He took out a pack of cigarettes and offered her one. In spite of herself, she felt flattered and giggled before refusing. She was beginning to relax.

"I don't know."

"Where's Stacy?"

"Oh her. Where do you think? With Will, naturally."

"Doesn't that boy ever do any baby delivering?"

Again she giggled, not sure why.

"I guess he'd rather plant his own," Johnny said, but that was over Caroline's head. Evidently sorry he had said it, he glanced at the door to see if anyone could have overheard. "So they left little Cinderella all alone."

"Alone? Gwen's here."

"Well—it's not the same thing. There they are, all of them having fun and you have to stay home."

21

Caroline looked puzzled and restless again. The friendliness she had felt at his mention of Buzzy and his offer of a cigarette was beginning to dissipate. "My mother and father aren't having fun. They're at meetings or something."

Sensing that he was losing ground, Johnny said briskly, "Where did your family live before they moved to Highlands, Carrie?"

Caroline, who detested that abbreviation of her name, moved to the couch and sprawled out, allowing her cotton robe to fall apart. She didn't notice his glance. "Let's see," she yawned. "I was born here. Stacy was born here—"

"Didn't she come here when she was a baby?"

"Nope."

Gwen came in quietly. "I think you ought to be in bed, Caroline."

Caroline, although she didn't care for the company, protested as a matter of course. "Bed! I don't have a bedtime in the summer."

"Sit up and pull that robe together."

"Treats you like a baby, doesn't she?" Johnny grinned.

"I'll tell Mr. Hubert you were here, Mr. MacLeod," Gwen said. "Caroline, please go upstairs."

"In a minute."

Gwen glanced at Johnny who smiled ingratiatingly but didn't move. Finally she went out.

"What were we saying? Oh yes. Where did your family live before they came to Highlands?" He searched for an ashtray, found a small china cup and flicked his ashes into it. Just then Gwen returned with a sewing basket and a canvas bag of socks. She sat down next to Caroline and began to darn. Johnny stared at her but she didn't look up.

"Could I have a cup of coffee?" he asked politely.

"Caroline, get Mr. MacLeod a cup of coffee," Gwen said placidly.

22

His eyebrows shot up and he grinned at Caroline, but she didn't seem to consider the request as strange as he did. Languidly she rose, stretched, and went to the kitchen. Gwen continued to darn. Neither one of them said anything.

"Cream and sugar?" Caroline shouted from the back of the house.

"No, thank you. Black," he shouted back and grinned as Gwen winced.

Caroline returned with the cup and saucer, but no tray or napkin. He thanked her, took one sip and said, "Well, I guess I'd better come back when the rest of the family is here."

"You didn't drink your coffee," Caroline said indignantly.

He downed a little more and rose. "Thank you—for the company and the coffee. Tell your father I was here."

Silently Gwen put down the sock and followed him to the door. She let him out and waited until the car started down the driveway. Then she went back to Caroline. "What a kook he is." Caroline yawned. "Let's watch television."

Saying no more about bedtime, Gwen picked up her paraphernalia and accompanied Caroline to the television room.

Johnny's next stop was at a house that was about a fifth of the size of the Huberts', and although it was on a pretty back road, it was neglected-looking. It was obvious that the owners had no outside help, and that they either didn't care or were unable to maintain it themselves. This time he had to knock. The door was locked.

A woman in her late fifties opened the door and her face collapsed when she saw him. She shut her eyes, and although she didn't invite him in, he walked past her.

The man was half sitting, half lying on the couch, reading the newspapers. His reaction to Johnny's presence was similar to the woman's, and like her, he didn't actually acknowledge the other's existence.

23

Again without being invited, Johnny sat down. Automatically he examined everything in the room: the smallness of it; the overcrowding, as though the furniture had once occupied a much larger space; the unpainted walls and the unvarnished woodwork. The only still expensive-appearing item was the Turkish rug.

"I told you," the man said, his voice quavering slightly, "I can't do it."

Restlessly Johnny picked up an ashtray and examined it. "May I have a drink?"

"We don't keep liquor in the house."

"Since when?"

"Since we can't afford it." He laced his hands and stared at the clotted veins.

Johnny grinned, a boyish grin, and said, "You're making me cry. Maybe I ought to send *you* a check."

Neither the man nor the woman had an answer for that pleasantry, so Johnny went on. "I have an idea. I'll do what those medical groups do—I'll ask my uh—clients to fill out income forms, and then the rich can subsidize the poor by paying according to an ascending scale. How about that?"

For the first time the woman spoke. "Did Jim Hostetter kill himself because of you?"

All the humor left Johnny's face—it was like watching a baby grow old and dangerous within a matter of seconds. "Okay —down to business. I didn't get your check this month."

"You've gotten enough from us," the woman said, her voice rising to the edge of hysteria. "It can't go on forever."

"Jeannette," her husband said, "he doesn't care about that."

"Right. On both counts. I don't care and it can't go on forever. Only as long as you live."

"Or *you* live," the woman whispered but the words were

erased by her husband's, "I don't have it. There's nothing left."

"There's always something left." Johnny looked around. "Sell the house. The furniture. Get a job."

"You know I can't work since I had the stroke."

"We have you to thank for that too," the woman said.

As though she were a fly, Johnny made a brushing motion in her direction. "You have a pension—something."

"It just pays for the taxes and food. As for selling the house—we have to live somewhere. There's a limit to how far you can push someone—" As though to himself, he added, "Jim Hostetter had one kind of limit, I have another. Someone else will have a third kind—"

Johnny wasn't listening. "Look, Mr. Brainard"—the "Mister" was a carry-over from when Johnny had been younger and Mr. Brainard had been a respected senior—"you can't have been living in Highlands all this time and sent Kitty to the schools you sent her to without having something more than a salary. Let's cut out the shit."

The woman stirred, but her husband held up his hand and she subsided. "*You* look. When my brother died, the family business dwindled to nothing. I can't work anymore. I sold what stocks and bonds I had when you started leeching on us."

Johnny folded his hands on top of his head, stretched his legs and examined the ceiling. "Balls. I can't show any favoritism to my clients. If you can't pay—"

"Get out of my house," Mrs. Brainard rasped, quivering with rage. "How dare you talk like that to us? I've had it. I won't take it any longer. You're a disgrace to your family, to your upbringing—"

"Yes, ma'am. You have my apology, ma'am. I forgot where I was. I guess the truth of the matter is that now that Kitty has Healey Mockridge all tied up, you don't care anymore. She's

25

safely married. Well—we'll see how the stuffy Healey Mock-ridge reacts to the truth about his sweet innocent wife.'' Lazily he got to his feet, stretched and buttoned his jacket. ''Or maybe Kitty will begin contributing to the kitty.'' His laugh and Mrs. Brainard's moan were simultaneous. ''Now you're going to start on Kitty,'' she whispered, but he paid no attention. He had an odd character quirk; an inability to feel anything beneath the surface. Even his anger never went deep. A part of what made the Homo sapiens different from the earlier primates had appar-ently been omitted from his makeup, and he couldn't be reached in the ordinary way.

''After all, both Kitty and Healey work.''

The man got laboriously to his feet, and his wife helped steady him. ''Kitty and Healey have joint accounts. He'd know if sizable sums were missing.''

''She can tell him she's helping her poor, destitute parents.'' He went to the door. ''Nothing wrong with that. I support *my* mother.''

The man was beginning to lose control too. ''*Me* ask Healey Mockridge for support? I never asked anyone for anything —Healey! A kid. I remember him when he was in diapers—''

Johnny shrugged. ''Sorry. In my business, I can't afford to make exceptions.''

''Get out—just get out—''

''That's what you said the first time I came to see you. Remember? But you reconsidered. Lucky I'm not vindictive. I'll give you a week. If I haven't heard from you by next Monday, I'll go to Healey—for a start.''

''Wh-what do you mean, for a start?'' The man sputtered, but Johnny, knowing a good exit line, went out and shut the door carefully behind him.

Back in the car, Johnny hesitated for the first time. He

glanced at his watch and saw that it was ten minutes past nine. With odd reluctance, considering his former brashness, he drove slowly, trying to make up his mind. He reached into the glove compartment, took out a flask and propped it under the arm which was controlling the wheel. Uncapping it with his free and, he took a quick swallow, waited and swallowed again before recapping it and returning it to the glove compartment.

In town, he parked in front of the drugstore and lit a cigarette. Finally he went inside, exchanged pleasantries with the pharmacist, bought shaving lotion and went out again. He had made up his mind.

Highlands was like the hub of a wheel with six spokes leading from it. He took a road which was different from the two leading to the Huberts' and the Brainards', stopping at a house that was much larger than the latter, but not nearly as perfect as the former. Nervously he lit another cigarette, and then, changing his mind, threw it into the grass. He walked to the door, swinging his arms aggressively, and examined the lawn with his nervous, almost tic-like habit of observing everything.

Again he walked in without knocking, and the Ketchums who were in the living room, looked up, a bit startled. "Hi, you all," he said jovially. "Doesn't anybody answer the door around here?"

Merrill was watching television and Elena was standing at an easel, apparently trying to reproduce a still life of peaches and grapes in a white bowl. She looked oddly posed, and although she couldn't have been expecting him, it was as though she was always prepared in case of a visitor.

With one wistful glance at the television set, Merrill jumped up, turned it off and said, "Well, hello there, stranger. How's the boy?"

"Stranger, he says," Elena mimicked. "And they both work for the same company!"

Johnny stepped back, lifted a finger and moved it back and

27

forth in front of the painting. "The surface texture isn't bad but the integral decorative factor is not in the cubist idiom."

"I'll idiom you," Elena said, making a stab at him with the brush. "Do you like? I'm giving them out as Christmas presents this year."

He put his head to one side. "Well, the synthesis of the blue period is merging with the classical echoes of the integration of form."

"How about a little nip?" Merrill asked, laughing.

"All rightie. Not *too* little though."

Merrill poured two stiff Scotch drinks, and just as he handed one to Johnny, Valerie Ketchum, a girl a year or two younger than Stacy Hubert, came into the room. She was fresh from the bath, her dark hair loose, and she was wearing an old robe. Unlike Caroline, she was self-conscious about her appearance, and she stopped in dismay. "Say—can't you whistle Dixie or something so a girl'd know you were here? I'd better get decent—"

"Not on my account, Valerie," Johnny said hastily. Although she was much more the right age for him than Caroline, of course, all of his gallantry was gone now and he was a little tongue-tied. "I—I'm only staying for a minute."

"Not with that drink you're not," Merrill said humorously. "That should be good for half an hour at least."

"Well make up your mind, people. Is he staying or isn't he? Tune in tomorrow and find out. Should Valerie change her clothing or shouldn't she? Should Johnny stay for half an hour or—"

"No, honestly. I have some business to discuss with your father, Val."

There was no doubt he was telling her to get out, and despite her surface breeziness, she flushed and said briskly, "Okay, okay already. You don't have to hit *me* over the head. I know when I'm not wanted. Is it all right if I get the newspaper?"

28

Elena squinted at her painting. "It's in the dining room."

"That's a good spot for it. Good night, you all. Don't get up on my account, Johnny." The last was a dig since he hadn't moved.

He smiled but didn't answer, taking a swallow of his drink instead.

When the clatter of her mules had disappeared, Merrill asked, "Well, boy, what can I do for you?" He had a jovial but not noisy personality, and even at his most jovial he always watched people carefully behind his thick eyeglasses. Johnny's interest in objects was matched by his interest in individuals.

"I like this room," Johnny said, glancing at the couch, the rug, the draperies, and finally at Elena's back. The three houses he had visited were an interesting study in contrasts—the Huberts' showed taste and money; the Brainards' taste; the Ketchums' money.

"So you dropped by to admire our living room," Merrill said. He wasn't one to let his curiosity go unheeded while making small talk.

"No, I'd like to discuss business." Again his glance strayed to Elena. Although he hadn't minded having Mrs. Brainard in the room, he had a curious reluctance to speak in front of Elena.

"Oh, oh," she said, trying to make it sound light but showing that she was slightly offended. "Do I have to join Valerie?" She waited for him to say it was all right for her to remain, but he took another sip of the drink. In dismay she glanced at her equipment.

"Come on, Johnny. We'll go to the library."

Library was a pretentious term for the small, pine paneled room without any books in it. The two of them sat down, and Johnny, to give himself courage, finished the drink. "Did you ever hear of a small company called Taubert Instruments, Mr. Ketchum?" he asked abruptly.

Merrill's face underwent a series of expressions. At first he

29

looked pleased, like a man who has been asked in a foreign city, "Do you know Ed Jones back in Sauk Centre, Minnesota?" and then, an expression of doubt crept in, as though he had just remembered something about his association with Ed Jones which he didn't want bruited about. Putting down his drink, he glanced at Johnny's empty glass but didn't offer to refill it. "Sure. I know the company. Don't tell me you want to leave us for them, Johnny."

Johnny, with an unfailing instinct, picked up the best piece of bric-a-brac on the table beside him—a gift from Angela Hubert—a porcelain bird.

"*Me* leave Narco Electronics? Not on your life, Mr. Ketchum."

"Well then?"

"I hear they're an up and coming company. Got a hell of a good contract lately"—he paused, lifted the empty glass and tried to drain it—"from us."

There was no doubt about Merrill's expression now. It was dangerous. Socially he was inept, a rather wistful snob. Physically he was awkward, short and round, not the magazine ad type of executive. But when it came to business, Merrill was a member of the élite. Tough to begin with, he had been tempered by almost thirty years of cutthroat company politics. He looked at Johnny as though the latter were a completely unqualified applicant sent into his office by mistake, and then, deliberately, he rose, went to the other room and returned with a drink for himself only.

Johnny hadn't moved all this time. Still admiring the porcelain bird, he said as though Ketchum had never left the room, "I have a copy of a letter from the president of Taubert Instruments addressed to you, and dated, of all things, three years from now. But there's no doubt of the authen—"

His startled eyes snapped up as Merrill slammed his glass on the table and rasped, *"What did you say?"*

30

"I said I have a copy—"

"How the hell could you have a copy of any letter addressed to me?"

"Suppose you wait and hear me out, Mr. Ketchum?"

"Hear you out? Damn it, I'll throw you out." His pale face was so clotted with blood now it seemed as if a vessel might burst through the skin at any moment.

Putting down the bird carefully, Johnny said, "That won't help, Mr. Ketchum," but his voice trembled faintly.

Like most bullies, Merrill could sense Johnny's fear. "What won't help? What the hell are you getting at?"

"They all talk that way at first."

"Who talks what way? I'll be damned if I spend any more time listening to this crap."

Johnny hesitated and then concluded that since Ketchum and Brainard were different kettles of fish, they needed different seasonings. "Mr. Hostetter, for instance."

"Mr. Host—" Merrill sat down. "Jim Hostetter—what does he have to do with this?"

"At first he got awfully mad and said he wouldn't pay."

"Wouldn't pay? Wouldn't pay what, damn you?"

Speaking slowly so that there wouldn't be any doubt as to his meaning, Johnny said, "He was like you. He got furious. I told him what would happen but he wouldn't believe me."

"What would happen?" Merrill repeated dazedly. He stared at Johnny as though he were changing form, evolutionizing in reverse into some lower form of life. "I don't get it. Jim killed himself."

"Yes. When he refused to pay up, I told his wife first. It was a warning. Then, if he had paid, I wouldn't have told anyone else. But he killed himself."

"Told his wife what?"

"I wouldn't tell you now," Johnny said piously. "The man's dead."

31

Merrill's brows drew together. "I bet I can make an educated guess."

"Let's get back to business, Mr. Ketchum."

"I always thought Jim had a little of the pansy in him. I guess it takes one to know one."

From the direction of an upstairs bedroom came the sound of a cuckoo clock. Then a spurt of laughter from Valerie, and the measured tones of Elena's voice.

Expressionlessly Johnny said, "I have a copy of a letter from the president of Taubert to you, dated three years from now"—apparently he had to begin at the beginning as though he had memorized the speech that way—"offering you a position as a consultant for them for fifty thousand dollars a year for five years."

Merrill couldn't work his vocal cords.

"I have one copy here and others in a safe place. Would you like to see it, Mr. Ketchum?"

Merrill didn't answer. Instead he lifted his drink and finished it.

"You have a lot of money, Mr. Ketchum. In addition to the fifty thousand in three years, you'll have a pension from Narco. I'm sure you'll take an early retirement even if you aren't sixty-five, in order to remove the conflict of interest. But anyway, what with stock options and all those side benefits, you're sitting in clover, Mr. Ketchum.

"Now, my job is lousy, Mr. Ketchum. You know what an assistant department head of advertising gets. And I have a mother to support. No side benefits, no stock options, no pensions—"

"And a 'friend' in the city to take care of?"

"I need a salary supplement, Mr. Ketchum. And you're going to contribute to it. Every month you'll send me—"

"*Every month!*" Merrill exclaimed incredulously as though that were the crux of the problem. Then he blinked, trying to remember who he was and who Johnny was. "I don't know what I'm doing here listening to you. Get out. There is no such letter, and if there was, what it said wouldn't be illegal, and if you ever tried—''

"Of course there's a letter, Mr. Ketchum. I thought a man like you wouldn't waste my time with silly denials." Johnny was gaining confidence, like a specialist warming up to a familiar job. "And I'll tell you how I know. I always keep my eyes open for prospective clients. For instance, I can almost smell people with a touch of larceny in them—''

Merrill made a sudden movement, but then he subsided and Johnny continued.

"—and I kept my eye on you. You were pretty anxious for Taubert to get that contract. That future date, by the way, Mr. Ketchum—suppose the president of Taubert dies? Well, I guess he had to protect himself—and we all have to gamble a little.

"Anyway I went to your office one day, Mr. Ketchum. Your secretary was down the hall. There was an envelope on her desk—no postal mark. It had been delivered by hand and it said personal on it. It made me curious. So I took it back to my own office—did you say something, Mr. Ketchum? No, well, I took it to my office and I opened it carefully.

"I think it was typed by the president of Taubert himself. At least there were no secretary's initials. And it was signed by him all right. And I told you the contents. So I simply zeroxed myself a few copies, resealed the envelope and put it back on the desk when your secretary was out to lunch. It was a little risky—she could have known about it and wondered where it was—but evidently the boy had put it down when she was out. Anyway, as I said, we all have to gamble a little."

"You filthy little—''

"You wouldn't like the other officers of Narco to know about the letter, would you, Mr. Ketchum? Or the stockholders. Or even your friends. I'll give you time to think it over. Actually

33

you surprise me. I would have thought that a smart businessman like you would show more uh—aplomb, but you're acting like the others. I'll telephone you next, let's see, next Tuesday. You ought to be able to make up your mind by then. Or you can let me know at the office. Or just send the first installment—I'll let you know the figure.''

While he spoke, he edged slowly to the door, as though knowing from experience that that was the best way. Still speaking, he reached behind him, opened the door and slid out, all in one movement. Merrill almost didn't realize he was gone until he heard the car motor.

III

"—under the st—back—gotta watch 'er," he mumbled, flinging an arm over the side of the bed and pulling up one knee. He
was lying face downwards, sprawled out, and he wore nothing
but the sheet twisted around him like a loincloth. He had started
disrobing at the doorway and had finished at the bed, leaving a
trail of jacket, tie, shirt, trousers, underwear, shoes and socks.

Because of the moonlight veneering the room with a pale gray
light, he was perfectly visible to the figure standing beside the
bed, but the latter was watching the open window. A car motor
had sounded in the distance, grown louder and roared so em-
phatically it seemed it would surely turn into the driveway, but
then it had shot past.

The man on the bed groaned and turned over on his back,
coiling the sheet with him, and the intruder spun back from the
window. The sleeper's face was almost extraordinarily ordinary—rounded on top and coming in, pear-like, towards the
chin. The eyes, even when open, were small, the nose a shade
too prominent, the mouth wide and the skin soft. And yet, the
aftereffect was abnormal. Like features on a television screen

35

where the last picture has burned a negative into the glass, the face couldn't be erased from memory. She stared at it with fascination, until the tops of the trees began to sway and the face was shredded by shadows.

Fantastically, considering the circumstances, she murmured a prayer. Then, bringing her hand out of the coat pocket, she lifted it, and the ice pick gleamed in the moonlight as she plunged it down with all her strength between the ribs and into the heart of the man lying on the bed. Something dropped to the floor from the coat pocket, but she noticed nothing.

Whatever had been on the bed a moment before was gone, but she remained rigid, as though waiting for an answer to some huge question. Instead, there was only a twitch and a faint sound to show what had happened. The victim's eyes hadn't even had time to open, and the ice pick had sealed the wound so that it didn't spurt. There were no more answers than if she had speared an insect.

It was the refrigerator motor starting up below that reminded her of what still had to be done. She opened the drawers, scattering the clothing on the floor, searched the closet and even looked under the bed. When she was sure that what she wanted wasn't there, she went down the hall to the stairs at the end. Feeling along the wall with gloved hands, she ascended to the attic and pressed the light switch. The enfeebled light revealed a dust-covered, cobwebbed room filled with old furniture, cardboard boxes crammed with odds and ends, mounds of old clothing. Again she searched, emptying boxes, overturning chairs, separating dresses and coats.

Again her efforts were in vain. She went down into the hallway, rubbing her hands together to rid the gloves of dust. Remembering something, she ran to the bedroom across the hall from the one with the body in it. This one was a woman's room. She didn't waste any time searching here but instead ran straight to the jewelry box on top of the vanity table, emptied the

36

contents into her pocket without examining them and then raced downstairs. She investigated the kitchen desk and, after glancing around the dining and living rooms, went down to the basement.

The light here revealed a larger version of the attic. She listened a moment and then went to the farthest end in order to cover the room systematically. The clock upstairs struck the half hour and she consulted her watch. Then she began taking down the boxes in the rear. There was a foot locker filled with yellowed, crocheted baby sweaters, booties, shoes, hats, a christening dress; fruit crates crammed with blankets, women's clothing of an indeterminate period, even nightgowns; corrugated boxes packed with picture albums, old checkbooks, newspaper clippings, ancient Christmas cards, a boy's school papers and report card, paid bills, invitations to dances, locks of hair, names of contributors to fashionable charities, dentist and doctor reports, everything except what the murderer wanted.

Suddenly a car motor sounded again, but this time it turned off almost overhead. A door slammed.

For a moment the figure examining the papers froze. Then she jumped to her feet, glanced around and turned off the light. She hid under the stairwell.

Above, the kitchen door opened and someone came in. Apparently whoever it was noticed nothing amiss and the footsteps receded towards the front of the house.

Instantly the murderer darted up the stairs as soundlessly as possible, peered into the kitchen and then tiptoed across it. The door was unlocked, as before.

The interlaced branches of the trees seemed like phalanxes of beings with clasped hands, closing in to prevent her escape. Near the house, the shadows were blurred, but under the sky, the bushes were sharply outlined like children's cutouts. Nothing moved in the whole deserted landscape, and the moonlight gave it the pallid appearance of a lifeless planet.

She ran to the street, glanced up and down, and when she saw no one, raced to the car she had left hidden by a group of trees where the dirt road began. She started up without turning on the lights.

Trying not to drive too quickly in case someone was awake and would remember the sound of a speeding car, she turned on the lights. Instantly she braked, mistaking a shadow for a tangible object. She was breathing heavily by the time she turned into her own driveway.

She left the car outdoors and let herself into the house quietly. She could still smell the dinner they had eaten that evening, a lifetime ago. Hanging up the coat, she tiptoed to her own room. Her nightclothes had been hidden underneath.

She did not hear a door shut quietly as she went to bed, because just then the police siren blasted through the distant town.

IV

When she woke up, Stacy remained still for a time, looking at the French windows leading to her own balcony. They were just flushed with dawn. She lay quietly, her face relaxed, and then something came into it, some awareness which puckered her skin, making the wide-awake face years older than the half-awake one. She listened, but there was nothing to hear except the twitterings of the chickadees, robins and sparrows. Reaching over her head, she turned on the bed lamp. Instantly the French doors sprang into a life of their own—straight ahead was a reflection that didn't seem possible. It was of a door, a dark rectangle hovering over the tops of the trees, and leading to a strange, tantalizing room, just beyond her grasp. She watched the door to nowhere, and then, impulsively, got up and went to the balcony. The door disappeared.

She stood on the balcony, watching two jays take possession of the birdhouse. Then, silently, she pattered across the floor to the door and opened it. She went down the curving staircase to the huge hall and into the cloakroom. Pushing aside the other coats, she found an old, soiled polo coat. She examined the pockets and found nothing but a paper tissue and a rubber band. Then she turned the coat slowly, scrutinizing the outside. A small twig was clinging to the hem and she took it off, unlocked the front door, and threw it away.

Standing under the portico, she watched the mist clinging to the tops of the trees, the rabbit chewing on dandelion leaves far down on the field, the jay swooping and scolding overhead. The air was delicious, and she might have remained indefinitely if the daily gardener hadn't driven up just then. She waved at him and ran upstairs.

For no reason, she buried her face in her pillow and waited to see how long she could stand it. Then she took deep gulps of air though she had been in real danger of suffocating. As she lifted her head, she caught sight of the local weekly newspaper, *The Town Crier*, on the bedside table, and she picked it up to read an item she had already seen.

James Hostetter, 46, vice-president in charge of industrial and public relations of the Corrigan Chemical Corporation, shot himself yesterday afternoon while sitting in his car in front of his house on Route 418. He was found by a neighbor, Richard Stenthal, who was returning from work at the time.

Mr. Hostetter's wife, Joan, could give no reason for the suicide, and no note was found. According to Mrs. Hostetter, her husband, Mr. Hostetter, had been in excellent health.

Mr. Hostetter is also survived by a son, Roger, 16, a student at St. Paul's School, and a daughter, Sherry, who is in the third form in Highlands Country Day School.

Chewing her lip, Stacy put the newspaper back on the table and went to the bathroom to shower. When she came out, she put on a sport dress and went down to the kitchen. The coffee was beginning to percolate when Caroline came in, still in curlers and pinned-together pajamas. Stacy eyed her sister as she lit a cigarette.

"Well, I can't help it," Caroline said defensively.

"What?"

"Just because I have a few pimples—"

"Caroline, do you know Roger Hostetter?"

"You mean the one whose father killed himself?"

"Yes."

"Nope."

"You never saw him around?"

"Well—Eunice's sister goes with him, I think. Actually, though, she says he's a creep. She's crazy about his room-mate."

"Who's crazy about his roommate?" Both girls turned to look at their father. His large frame was encased in an outfit that looked like what the well-dressed man should wear while playing golf. The gray sport shirt, yellow sweater and gray flannel slacks were a startling contrast to Caroline's ou~~~ ~~ ~~~~ made Stacy look a bit shabby.

"Eunice's sister. She's crazy about Roger's room.ate."

"*I'm* crazy about my housemate," Frank said and pinched Caroline's bottom.

"Dad, don't be *gross*," Caroline said furiously.

Gwen came in and started frying bacon. She wore a pink and white uniform, and the three of them made Caroline resemble an orphan.

"I've been meaning to tell you," Frank said to her, "I think that if we manage our finances very carefully, we can afford a new pair of pajamas for you, Caroline."

Caroline looked down. "What's wrong with these? I had to pin them. You wouldn't want them to fall, would you?"

"You have three pairs you haven't even worn," Gwen reminded her gently.

"Waste not, want not," she said virtuously. "Besides, these are the only comfort—" She broke off as the daily cleaning woman arrived, and with her, Jelly Bean, who flew at Caroline as though he hadn't seen her for a month. His wet paws left marks all over her pajamas. To make sure the topic of conversation didn't return to her appearance, Caroline said, "Did you hear funny noises last night?" Automatically she began helping Gwen set the table.

Stacy, who was helping too, stopped and said, "What kind of noises?"

"I don't know—all kinds—a car, I think—the door—"

"Why didn't you do something?"

"My theory is that if someone is robbing the house, let them. I'm more valuable than the silver."

"You imagined it," Frank said. "Stace—how about some golf this mornir..."

"Nobody asked me," Caroline pointed out.

"You wouldn't want to be seen with a *gross* father. How about it, Stace?"

"I can't, Dad. This is my day at the hospital. Did I tell you about—"

"You mean I have to play with Caroline?"

"Gee, thanks a heap. What a gracious invitation." Nevertheless, she hurriedly filled a bowl with cornflakes and went to the shelf for sugar. "Whose are these?" she asked, holding up a crumpled pack of Camel cigarettes and an industrial lighter.

"—sure she knows she has cancer," Stacy was saying, "but she won't—"

"Stacy, are these your cigarettes?"

"What? No. She won't admit it. When I go—" Stacy stopped and looked at the cigarettes again. Slowly she said, "They belong to Johnny MacLeod. At least, I think he's the only one we know who smokes Camels."

"That reminds me, Dad," Caroline said, "did Johnny ever get to see you? He was here Monday."

"He didn't leave them Monday," Gwen said. "I'd have seen them yesterday—" She broke off.

"He dropped by last night." Frank's voice was casual.

"What a goon he is. He wouldn't leave me alone—"

"What do you mean he wouldn't leave you alone?" Frank asked sharply.

"Oh—when he came Monday, he insisted on my coming down. I was in my pajamas—"

"Why did he want to see you?"

"Gee, I don't know. He asked me to come down—"

"What did you talk about?"

"This and that. He called me Cinderella and said it was a shame all of you going out and leaving me alone—" She broke off as the telephone rang. "I'll get it." Deliberately she waited for it to ring three times before picking it up. "Hello?" Her face went pink and she giggled self-consciously. "Wait—I have to change phones."

Running to the other room, she shouted, "Hang up, some-body."

"Were you in the room when Johnny was here?" Frank asked Gwen as Stacy picked up the pack of Camels and dropped it in her pocket. The two of them started on their bacon and eggs.

"He asked her where you all lived before coming to High-lands," Gwen said expressionlessly.

Frank watched her a moment. "What did she say?"

Before Gwen could answer, Caroline was back. "Dad—oh Dad, could you leave me at the club for lunch?"

"Got a date?"

"Yes, as a matter of fact."

"Who is it?"

"Buzzy."

43

"Buzzy who?"

"Oh, Dad—honestly. How many Buzzys are there?"

Stacy finished her breakfast swiftly and went to the garage. Two cars stood there, an old Ford station wagon and a Bentley, but ignoring those, she went out to the car parked in front of the garage, a Mercedes. She was examining the front seat and floor when she heard Caroline shouting, "Stacy—call for you."

Dusting off her hands, she went back to the kitchen and picked up the telephone, a familiar flicker of excitement shooting through her. "Hello?"

"Can't have a peaceful breakfast," Frank muttered, leaving the room. On the whole, however, he sounded a little smug about his daughters' popularity.

"Stacy?" It was Kitty, and Stacy sat down, the excitement draining out. "Did you hear what happened? Is your radio tuned to the local station?"

"No—what happened?"

"Johnny MacLeod was murdered last night!"

V

"Are you still with me?" Kitty asked, but Stacy was watching something taking place on the lawn. The black and white cat which belonged to a family down the road was stalking a bird. His long body slithering close to the ground, he was watching the grass under the oak tree. Above, a cardinal swooped to a tree branch, and in the shadows below, Stacy saw another cardinal tugging at the ground and pulling out a long, struggling worm. Just then the cat pounced.

Dropping the telephone with a slam, Stacy ran to the door. "Get away," she screamed at the cat. "Scat." She raced down the lawn, shouting. She could see the back of the cat, claws and teeth hidden as they ripped. Sending him flying with a kick, she looked down.

She was too late. Most of the bird's feathers had been torn off and its throat was open, oozing blood. Above, in the tree, its mate chattered in agony. Stacy was afraid she would be sick. Turning, she went back to the house, and it was only then that she remembered the call. The receiver was dangling from its cord and emitting impatient sounds.

"Kitty, I'm sorry—"

"I didn't know you cared that much for Johnny MacLeod. Are you all right? I heard this crash—"

"Johnny MacLeod! I don't know what—a cat was tearing a bird apart on the lawn and I ran to—"

"You know something? You're impossible. Utterly, absolutely impossible. If I didn't know you from the year one—I just told you someone was murdered. Aren't you the least bit interested?"

"Yes, of course. I mean—what happened?"

"He was stabbed last night with an ice pick. Right through the heart. Mrs. MacLeod came home last night and found—"

"I thought Mrs. MacLeod is never home on Tuesday night." After it was out, Stacy wished she had kept quiet.

"Yes, that's it. Exactly!" Kitty spoke so quickly the words were almost unintelligible. "The police think the murderer must be someone who knows the MacLeods because he picked the one night she always spends with her cousin Mrs. Taylor—"

"Then, how come—"

"She was having three tables of bridge for lunch today, and so instead of spending the night with her cousin, she just had dinner there and came home so that she could get up early and prepare lunch. Which, of course, eliminates everyone who was expected at her house today—"

"What? Why?"

"You're just not functioning this morning. Don't you see? Johnny was probably killed by someone who wouldn't know Mrs. MacLeod was having a lunch today and would be home—"

"Even the people having lunch in her house today might not know she came home last night because of it."

"Well—maybe."

"Anyway, are you serious? Do you really think it was someone who was a friend of the MacLeods?"

46

"Enemy would be more like it. How should I know? understand some jewelry was stolen, so I suppose it could have been some wild kid who knew Mrs. MacLeod was out on Tuesday and that Johnny is generally potted any night of the week."

"Then why was Johnny killed?"

"I guess—maybe Johnny woke up caught him and the thief panicked."

"Yes," Stacy said. "That's obably it."

"But why would a thief carry an ice pick?"

"Oh—just a weapon. You know—like some of them carry guns."

"Well—I thought I'd tell you. Though for all the interest you've shown—the next time I have news I'll call Caroline."

"It isn't that I'm not sorry about Johnny, Kitty—"

"You don't have to go *that* far. *I'm* not the least bit sorry about Johnny."

Stacy hesitated. "You're right. I'm *not* functioning very well this morning. That poor little bird—"

"Oh spare me. That bird again! Tell me something, Stace, do you still have funeral services for all your dead fish and mice?"

"It seems to me, Kitty my girl, *you* were the one who used to read the service."

"Yes, but *I* outgrew it. I think I'll call someone more responsive. See you later."

When she had hung up, Stacy looked out again and saw that the cat was still working on the mutilated corpse. She turned away and went upstairs. Knocking gently, she entered her mother's room. Angela was just waking up. Her neat gray-brown hair in a nightcap, she was on her side, legs curled up and her cheek in her hand. She opened her eyes when Stacy came in, coughed, groaned tiredly and sat up. "Why is everybody up so early?"

Through the open window Stacy saw her father and sister

47

drive away. "Johnny MacLeod was murdered last night."

"Murdered! Johnny MacLeod? What are you talking about?"

Stacy related what Kitty had said, keeping her coverage neutral like an honest reporter anxious not to let his own views show. While she talked, Angela got out of bed, went to the connecting bathroom, washed, and then disappeared into her dressing room. When she emerged, bathed, made up, hair combed and figure encased in a tweedy-looking cotton, she appeared five years younger. Briskly she said, "I'd better call Harriet."

"Do you think you ought to disturb her? I mean, at a time like this?"

"Stacy! I can't ignore the fact that her son was murdered. I can see me meeting her on the street one day and saying, 'Oh, by the way, I heard Johnny was killed the other night—' "

"But she has a cousin—and close friends—"

"Don't be ridiculous. Certainly we're not bosom companions, but we *are* friendly." As her mother lifted the bedroom telephone, Stacy took a stick of gum from her pocket, shoved the wrapping paper back in her pocket, and began to chew. She went downstairs, hearing her mother say, "Harriet? It's Angela. I can't tell you how—"

Stacy waited near the French windows in the sitting room, as though expecting something. Her body tensed as Angela's footsteps sounded on the stairs. Angela came in, looking dazed.

"What's the matter?" Stacy demanded.

"Well, what could I do? *She* suggested it."

"Suggested what?"

"I asked her if there was anything I could do to help. It's the sort of thing anyone would say, isn't it? And do you know what she answered? She said she was afraid to stay alone and could she come here for a few days."

"What did you do?"

"Then she also asked if we could drive her to the funeral services and the cemetery afterwards. Apparently the police have the uh—body, but they'll uh—return it in time for the funeral on Friday."

"What did you do?" Stacy repeated.

"Well, what could I do? I said certainly."

VI

Three days after Johnny's funeral, Kitty received a note.

WHOEVER KILLED JOHNNY MACLEOD
WILL PAY FOR IT.

It was penciled carelessly on a piece of pad paper in block letters. It was as though whoever had written it didn't care if it was traced or not.

She sat in her car and stared at it incredulously for a few moments, and then the sensation of nausea set in. She fought against getting sick in the middle of town, and glanced over her shoulder, afraid someone was watching. As a matter of fact, she met the eyes of one of her students who was crossing in front of the car. Although he couldn't possibly have seen the note, she was sure that he had sensed something wrong with her face. She looked down at her lap for a moment and waited before examining the street. It was possible that whoever had sent it knew she picked up her mail in town every morning.

She saw Mrs. Newhouse going into the market, and farther

down, Willis Tobin getting into his car with the newspaper. Neither one of them was paying any attention to her. She sat in the car awhile longer, and then, instead of doing her errands, she drove straight home. Feverishly she changed from her shorts and shirt to a city knit, combed her hair, put on makeup and went back to the car.

She drove through town and out on the parkway, heading south. With sleep-walking intensity she paid no attention to her surroundings, and miles passed without her being aware of them. Her subconscious took over and she went past her destination. She found herself close to the shopping and theater sections, and saying a word which she couldn't remember ever having used before, she drove off the parkway at the next exit. She had to thread her way back through the depressing West Side streets and then head north again. Now and then she glanced at the directions on the slip of paper beside her. It had been in the old tan leather shoulder strap bag she had used back in boarding school, and for some reason she had never destroyed it.

It was coming back with crystal clarity, that distant day when her parents had made the first appointment, and she had sat between them, driving down, no one speaking. The sickness had risen in her throat, and her father swerved to the side of the parkway so that she could throw up. Her father's eyes had avoided hers, and he hadn't addressed a word to her the whole way. Thinking about it now, she had the same desire to throw up, without the same reason.

The section was becoming familiar. She went up Riverside Drive, past the old mansions, the apartment houses, the river, and it was like seeing a famous beauty whom age and time had turned into a whore. But her biggest shock at the time had been in seeing—not the decay, the filth, the deterioration—the doctor himself. A Puerto Rican.

She had turned to flee, but her father had grasped her arm in a cold, steely grip and said, "This is the doctor, Kitty."

She had said, "Dad, please—I want to go home—" but she might have been a bodiless, voiceless spirit for all the attention anyone had paid her.

"It will take three visits," the man had said.

That part had shaken her father. "You can't—can't you do it in one?"

"Your daughter's safety is important to you, isn't it?" He had been kind (his had been the only kindness she had encountered ever since the hideous knowledge had burst upon her) and young, and had had a pleasant voice. But she hadn't been able to respond to his kindness—only to his color. To her, doctors had always been portly friends of her parents, extremely old (which meant past forty), a little vague, and, of course, eminently white.

She had clung to her mother, appealing to her, and her mother had begun to cry. "You'll be glad, Kitty—think, when it's all over. You can go back to school—be like the other girls. No one will ever know. But if you don't, your whole life—"

"Mummy, I can't—please—"

In the end, she had done it. And the nightmare had never left her. The humiliating, filthy nightmare.

She saw the house then. Seven years had passed, but she recognized it immediately: the paradox of the wide street and magnificent view combined with the gnawing disintegration.

If she hadn't found a parking space almost immediately, she might still have changed her mind and driven home, but a car pulled away just as she drew up. She got out and the bile rose in her throat. At home she had considered the beige cotton knit dress the least conspicuous of her outfits, but here she would have been less conspicuous in the wildest print. She could feel the hostile stares examining her dress, her small-heeled shoes, her chamois gloves, her handbag. Actually I have very little money, she kept saying silently. Stories of rape and assault on the streets in midday rose in her mind.

Broken glass crunched under her shoes as she entered the badly lit, dirty hallway. Without having to think about it, she went up the steps, turned right and tried to breathe shallowly so as not to be nauseated by the smell of poverty. She turned the knob gingerly and went into the anteroom.

Nothing had changed. Certainly crime didn't pay, to judge by the two kitchen chairs, the frayed couch and the linoleum-covered floor. A prosperous doctor who had refused to help her had had a wood-paneled office on Park Avenue, leather-covered furniture, Louis XIV side tables, and what looked like a Klee on the wall.

There was no nurse, and the doctor himself came out of his office at the sound of the bell. He stopped in surprise, no recognition on his face.

If the office hadn't changed, he had. He looked as though many more than seven years had passed: there was gray in his hair and lines on his face.

"Do you have an appointment?" he asked politely.

"Please—may I see you for a moment? It won't take long."

The slight alteration in his expression was so fleeting she wasn't sure she hadn't imagined it, but she said defensively, "It isn't—I just have to *talk*."

He stepped back, holding the door for her, and she preceded him into the smaller inner office, which held only two chairs and a desk.

When they were both seated, she stared at a spot midway between the desk and the door to the examination room and said, "I was here seven years ago—I was very young. You performed an illegal operation for me."

"I remember," he said expressionlessly. "You've changed."

"I'm not here for the same reason," she went on and felt her face get hot. "As a matter of fact, I'm married—I wish I *could* have a baby, but—I didn't come to talk to you about that. I have a question to ask you."

"Nothing I did could have prevented your having a child now."

The outer bell sounded and she jumped. "Are you expecting a patient? Are you in a hurry?"

"That's all right."

But Kitty hesitated, looking at the door to the anteroom.

"No one can hear us," he said patiently.

Kitty pulled off her gloves and then carefully began putting them on again. "I'm not blaming you about not having a child—the doctor said, he assured me there was no physical reason—it's something else. It's crazy to ask you this now, after all this time. I've wanted— But my father said no, don't make it worse."

"I'm afraid I don't understand."

"I'm not being very— What happened was, well, shortly after it was all over, someone began blackmailing us—" She looked up and was surprised to see that he had shut his eyes. "Are you all right?"

He opened his eyes and nodded.

"I wanted to ask you how anyone could have found out. I mean it was to your interest to keep it quiet. And of course the uh—father wouldn't tell anyone—he didn't even know—so how did anyone find out? My father didn't want to ask you. He didn't want to get involved any further. So he just paid."

"So did I."

"What did you say?"

"I said so did I."

She looked at him uncomprehendingly a moment, and then, despite her resolution to be cautious, burst out, "Johnny Mac-Leod blackmailed *you* too?"

54

"I paid him a certain amount monthly for protection."

"*Paid?* You know he's dead?" She was wary again.

He hesitated for a moment and then reached into his desk. To her surprise he had a copy of the Highlands *Town Crier*.

"Where did you get that?"

"I have had a subscription ever since MacLeod began —getting protection money."

"Why?"

"I was— I wanted to know what I could about his home, his— It's hard to say. I felt I ought to know."

She stared a moment, then shook her head, glanced at the outer door and said, "I came to find out how he got his information."

"Why now? As you said—after all this time—"

"Because someone else knows."

"What!" For the first time his air of reserved weariness evaporated and he smacked the chair against the wall and got to his feet. "How do you know? Are you being blackmailed again?"

She stared at him in surprise, but his obvious agitation had the odd effect of making her feel more at ease. "I received a note in the mail today—here. I have it with me." She handed it over and he stared at it a long time. Finally he returned it.

"My God—and I thought—" For a moment he rubbed his chin, and then abruptly he asked, "Who do you think it is?"

"I—well—I have an idea, but I'm not sure. What I want to know is, how did Johnny find out in the first place?"

"I'll tell you in a minute. But first, I've got to know—if it starts up again—"

"I don't think it will. That is, I think this person wants revenge more than money."

"Revenge. Then it's someone close. The newspaper said he was survived by his mother. Do you think his mother sent this?"

"Oh Lord, I'm making such a mess— Yes, I do."

55

"Then she must have known about his blackmailing activities."

"Well—I didn't think about that. Yes, I guess she must have. She's a funny woman. She's the kind of person who hides things from herself. If a fact is unpleasant, she pretends it isn't there. I mean, she could have known and not known. Does that make sense?"

He looked at her helplessly.

"She would know underneath, but gloss it over in her own mind. I can see her telling herself it isn't really so bad, those people can afford it. He's doing them a favor by not telling and so forth. Besides, she probably liked the things he could buy her. And there's something else. She couldn't control him. She never could. She knew if she fought him, he'd probably walk out and leave her. There's another little character trait he had—which she may or may not have known about, but she must have suspected—and she simply has to ignore it."

"That note—it doesn't actually say she knows about the abortion. It sounds as though she suspects Johnny MacLeod was blackmailing you but not the reason."

"That's—well, that's possible. She may be fishing around. You haven't told me how Johnny found out."

He watched her a moment and then said tiredly, "Not too long after you were here, MacLeod came. I don't know how he got my name—these things have a way of circulating—and he was obviously one who was alert for all possibilities of blackmail. He had a girl with him. She was pregnant, but I'm sure he was not the father—"

"So am I," said Kitty grimly. "Go on."

"He had simply found out she was in trouble and offered to help her—he's probably blackmailing her too—" He wanted to pace, but the office was too small and he had to sit down again. He rubbed the top of his head. "Well, where was I? Oh. Anyway, the last time MacLeod came with the girl, he stayed in

56

this office. I came out of the examining room unexpectedly and I found him at the desk. He wasn't even embarrassed. There he was, going through all my papers—''

"That was Johnny all right."

"—and he looked up and smiled and said, 'I can't help this nosy streak I have. It's a disease.' At the time I didn't know he had taken anything. I just thought he was peculiar—I see all kinds. Anyway, when he was gone I saw that the check your father had sent me was gone too. I had gotten it in the mail the day before and put it in the desk—''

"I don't understand—''

"I didn't know Johnny MacLeod's real name at the time or where he lived. I was helpless. I thought he was simply trying to cash it. Then, about a week later, I got the check back. He'd photostated it, and this time he gave me his real name and address. He pointed out that a check for four hundred dollars from a man like your father to a doctor like me might lead to a lot of unpleasant questions and, well, you know the rest.''

"I see." She got up and began smoothing the gloves again. "I don't think—that is, if Harriet MacLeod had found the check, she might have made the threat more definite. She must simply suspect Johnny was blackmailing me—and yes, she must be fishing—hoping I'll betray myself, get scared, something. She adored Johnny. If there ever was an adoring mother— How could he have turned out so badly?'' Drearily they both looked at one another. It was odd, Kitty thought, that they were almost treating one another like old friends with a shared problem. She had nearly forgotten what for her had been his salient feature. "Well, I haven't solved anything, have I? Anyway, I just wanted to find out. Thank you.''

He followed her to the anteroom. An elderly Negress sitting on the couch stared at Kitty, and Kitty's momentary sensation of kinship with the doctor disappeared.

She drove quickly, anxious to leave behind the dirt and the

57

poverty and the ugly memories. Although she knew that the fastest vehicle in the world couldn't accomplish what she wanted, she longed to be back in her own safe surroundings again. I'll go to the club, she thought, and have a swim and I'll talk Healey into taking me out. She was back on the West Side Drive, and the breeze from the open window lifted her hair and cooled her neck. She was almost feeling normal again when a car honked at her. Thinking someone wanted to pass, she swung over into the slow lane. And then Elena Ketchum drove past, waving gaily.

Her problems engulfed her again. Mrs. Ketchum. She had thought she was in a different world from Highlands, and there was Mrs. Ketchum. Had she seen at what point Kitty had re-entered the highway? Would she suspect anything? Although she knew it was ridiculous, she was sick and oppressed. She felt as though Big Sister had been watching her.

VII

What had made Kitty look at her so oddly, Elena wondered. First she had stared blankly, and then her eyes had widened with—with what? Were there rumors going about in town about the Ketchums? Had Kitty heard something?

Almost tearfully she thought, but I've always liked Kitty; I've always been nice to her. And why hadn't Kitty telephoned to ask Elena if she wanted to go to the city with her, when she knew Elena hated to drive? Generally she did. She had always been deferential to Elena because Healey worked for Narco too—many steps down from Merrill's position, of course.

I wish I'd never gone to New York, she thought disconsolately, glancing at the package beside her. She had always shopped locally, but recently she had overheard two women cattily suggesting that she ought to consult Angela about decorating. Angela had arranged entry for her to several "decorator" houses, and she had collected a number of swatches, all of which she disliked. Irrationally, she was annoyed with Angela.

Merrill's car was parked in the driveway when she got home, and alarmed she ran in. "Merrill? Where are you?"

"He's in the library, Mrs. Ketchum," the maid called from the direction of the dining room.

She went straight in and found him on the floor surrounded by the contents of his desk. "What in the world are you doing?"

"What does it look like I'm doing?"

"What a mess. Why are you home so early? I would have called your office when I was in town, but I know you hate to be disturbed—"

"That's right," he snapped. "I hate to be disturbed."

She started to answer sharply, but his face warned her. She went out, put away her things and spoke to the maid about dinner. Finally she fixed a tray with cheese and crackers, drinks and napkins and went back to the library. He accepted the drink without comment.

When five or six minutes had passed, she ventured a question. "What are you looking for?"

"I'm not looking for anything. I'm making sure there's nothing here that can ever interest anyone."

"But Johnny's dead." It was the wrong thing to say. She lost the ground the drink had won her.

"You know something? You're not very bright."

"The door's shut. Or do you think there are hidden mikes around?"

"That's not as farfetched as you think. Some of the stories I've heard— Anyway just don't *think* like that, much less talk like that."

"I feel as though I'm living in Russia. Have you cleaned up the bank vault too?"

"Yes, as a matter of fact."

"But there was nothing really illegal—"

"Will you shut up?"

"No, *you* shut up. We're in our own house in our own town in the U.S.A. If we can't talk here— There *was* nothing illegal about it, was there?"

"Who knows what's legal or illegal? It's a damn fine line. Besides, that's not the point. The point is that one little whisper, one little hint, I'm out on my ass. Of course if you don't mind giving up this house and a maid and four or five fur coats and I don't know how many diamond—"

"If I weren't a lady— It's just me, is it? And what about *your* five or six club memberships and the trip to South America and, and—the best set of golf clubs in the country—"

"Keep your voice down." His own anger began diminishing as hers increased. "Anyway, as you said, Johnny's dead. Amen." He finished up and went back to the living room. He was still burning papers in the fireplace when Valerie returned from work. "Hello, you two. Why the conflagration?"

"I'm burning my old love letters."

"At *your* age you should be proud of them."

"It's time you got married," her mother said. "You don't have enough to occupy your mind."

"Well, *I'm* ready, willing and able. Do you have any candidates?" At that moment the telephone rang. "And there's one now," she added. "These candidates. They won't leave me alone for a minute. Hello?" Then her expression changed. Her eyes widening, she said, "Hello? Who is this?"

Her mother and father watched her as she hung up. "Who was that?" Merrill asked.

"Search me."

"What do you mean, search me? Who was it, damn it?"

"You don't have to bite my head off. It was a kind of whispery voice—"

"A whispery voice!" Elena exclaimed.

"—and it said, 'What did Johnny MacLeod know about Merrill Ketchum?' "

"What!" her father exploded, and at the same time her mother jumped to her feet and grabbed her arm. "Keep your voice down," Elena rasped, glancing in the direction of the kitchen. "Don't you have any sense at all?"

"What did I—I mean, all I did was answer. It was some kind of a joke, wasn't it?"

"God, when will you get some sense?"

"But really— I mean, it sounded like one of those movie magazines: 'Who was seen with what actor at which night club last night?' "

"Except that in this case, Johnny MacLeod happens to be dead," her mother said furiously. "I don't want you to ever repeat one word—"

"All right, already. I promise not to stand in front of the drugstore and shout, 'What did Johnny—' "

"Valerie!"

"You're still behaving as though I were twelve. 'Now, big ears, no repeating what you hear at the table.' "

"That's enough."

Valerie walked out, heading for the stairs. When she was gone her mother and father were silent for a while, each sipping thoughtfully. Finally Merrill said, "Damn, damn, damn."

Hesitantly Elena said, "Whoever killed Johnny certainly was sloppy."

Merrill, getting up to pour another drink, spun around. "What did you say?"

"I mean—it wasn't a clean job. There's been a loose end left around. What I'm trying to say is, if Johnny *was* killed because he was blackmailing someone, well, the murderer should have made sure there were no incriminating papers—"

"You think someone else got hold of Johnny's papers?" He finished pouring the Scotch and then said slowly, "No. If this other character had the papers he wouldn't be asking questions. He'd know the answers."

"Yes, but obviously someone suspects something."

Putting his head back, Merrill swallowed a third of his drink. "Maybe if we're lucky, there'll be another murder."

62

VIII

From down the hall, Stacy heard Caroline saying, "I do. I was born right in this house. I mean, not exactly in the house, because I was born in the hospital actually, but we were living in this house."

For a moment the words meant nothing to Stacy. She had a headache, and since she so seldom had one, she tried to trace it to something concrete. Like Johnny's funeral. It was the first one she had ever attended and it still troubled her because no one had cried except Mrs. MacLeod. Even the cadence of the words, "Yea, though I walk through the valley of the shadow of death, I will fear no evil: for thou art with me; thy rod and thy staff they comfort me," produced no response in her or, apparently, in anyone else.

Johnny had entered the world thirty-one years before, he had gurgled and toddled like other babies, played baseball like other boys, gone to school like other children, and then he had taken a strange turn, a turn towards evil. And there had been no one to mourn him—not even his "friend" from the city—except his mother.

Thinking of his mother, she felt worse. Mrs. MacLeod had

only been with them for a few days, but the weight of her presence had been oppressive. She did nothing offensive, said nothing offensive, but she always seemed to be listening and waiting. Without being abnormal, nothing was normal. The family did everything they would have done if she hadn't been there, and yet, they all felt encumbered by her. She didn't even discuss her bereavement. If anything, her conversation consisted almost entirely of gossip—she would mention something about a person and then wait a moment, as though to see if any additional information was forthcoming.

"Take a child like yourself," she was saying now. "You know so little about your family history. A person ought to be interested in his ancestors. For instance, I bet you know absolutely nothing about your grandparents."

"They're dead."

"So is George Washington, but you're interested in *him*, aren't you?"

"Now that you mention it," Caroline said, giggling appreciatively at her own humor, "not really."

"You don't even know where your mother and father lived before they came to Highlands."

Stacy felt large and unwieldy, as though she had gained fifty pounds overnight. She couldn't move.

"Sure I do. They had an apartment in the city."

"Where?"

"Oh—I don't know. Park Avenue, I guess," she said, mentioning the only address she knew.

"Well, I bet you don't know where they were born," Harriet said softly, as though trying to persuade Caroline to modify her voice by setting her an example.

"Ohio, I guess. Somewhere in the middle." Everything west of New York and east of California was the "middle" to Caroline.

Stacy, still phlegmatic, wondered why she could hear so

well. Then she remembered that she had gotten into the habit of leaving her door open every night—a throwback to when man had to sleep with part of his brain alert to danger.

"Ohio? I thought it was Illinois—Chicago."

A nerve was touched. Shaking off the weight, Stacy jumped out of bed, grabbed her robe and hurried down the hall. "Good morning," she said brightly, entering Caroline's room. "What are you early birds doing?"

"Catching worms. What else?" Caroline said, overcome by her own humor again.

"Late birds get the steak, you know," Stacy said, a little wildly. "I thought I heard something about, uh, Ohio."

"Oh, that." It was Harriet who answered. "I've always been interested in people. You know—their heritage and background. It's a hobby of mine. Some people collect things, you know, like your mother, but I collect facts."

"Like Johnny," Stacy said buoyantly and then added quickly, "I mean there are facts and facts. Some facts add to the total sum of human understanding and well-being, and other facts—they're meaningless things designed to cater to the low, prying instincts of certain— Did you ever hear of President Arthur?"

"What did you say about Johnny before?" Harriet asked and Caroline groaned, "We sure are going in for history this morning. First Washington and now Arthur."

"President Arthur said— Do you know who he was?"

"A president?" asked Caroline.

"Yes. How did you know? Well, when he was asked by this woman if he drank, he said, 'Madame, I may be President, but my private life is my own goddamned business.' "

"Stacy! There's no need—and in front of your little sister."

"Well," Stacy continued, clapping her hands together in somewhat hysterical exuberance, "what's everybody having for breakfast?"

"I'll have two eggs," Caroline said, "four strips of bacon, two popovers and marmalade. Where were Mother and Dad born, Stace?"

"Why do you want to know? Are you writing a family history?"

"Mrs. MacLeod asked me. Did you know that Mrs. MacLeod's family practically founded Highlands? But they lost their money and lots of rich people came and bought up their land. It's sort of sad."

"Shirt sleeves to shirt sleeves," Stacy said bouncily. "Don't put on something awful like last week. Wear your plaid."

"I don't want to go to church. Why can't I stay home with Dad?"

"Dad's a Godless man. Hurry."

"Stacy, dear, don't talk that way, even as a joke. What you said about shirt sleeves is right. Now it's your father's turn to have the money. And he's been very generous with it, too. I mean, donating that new wing to the hospital. And the hours he puts in for the Red Cross and the Community Chest! It's wonderful. Of course, he doesn't have to work for a living, so he has lots of time. How did he make all his money, by the way?" She added the last so offhandedly, Stacy was almost caught off balance. But she caught hold of the door knob and sighed. "Oh dear, finance is beyond me, Mrs. MacLeod." Her voice was so feathery by now it almost took off. "Besides, he didn't really make it. It came down through his grandfather or some such thing. Caroline, get dressed."

Politely, Stacy waited for Mrs. MacLeod to precede her out of Caroline's room, and then she shut the door firmly. She accompanied the older woman to the guest room and then went back to dress. Once she was alone, her frothiness evaporated. In almost feverish haste, as though afraid Mrs. MacLeod might corner Caroline again, she dressed in a dark silk ribbon dress and put on a hair band instead of a hat.

It was she who drove Harriet, Angela and Caroline to church. Many people were away or playing golf and the church was only about half filled. Stacy's attention kept wandering and it was only gradually that she became aware of what Dr. Trowbridge was saying.

"—who would never consider throwing a stone in a neighbor's window, for instance, would think nothing of gossiping. In other words, he will not destroy his neighbor's property, but he *will* destroy what is infinitely more precious, his neighbor's reputation."

Stacy felt her skin growing hot. She stared at her lap, afraid of meeting someone's eyes.

" '—shalt not bear false witness against thy neighbor.' How many of us violate this every day of our lives? He who maligns his neighbor maligns God, for is not man made in God's image?" Dropping his voice from the oracular to the intimate, he continued, "It seems to me that one of the few precepts of psychology which is valid is the one of projection. In other words, one sees one's own sins in another person. How often have you criticized a friend for something you yourself have done at one time?"

Once she had been wrestling on the floor with Caroline and Caroline who had been only three at the time had kicked her accidentally in the stomach. All the breath had left her lungs so that for a moment she felt in danger of suffocating. She had spent a dreadful moment trying to catch her breath, and when it had come, it had caused her agony. She felt that way now. She was sure he was referring to gossip he had heard about the Huberts.

She remained in her seat, pretending to search for a glove, until nearly everyone had filed out. Finally she got up and hurried towards the parking lot.

"Stacy! Where are you going?" It was Angela.

"Home."

"We're staying for coffee."

"Mother, please—"

"Stacy," her mother said, a faint smile at the outer edges of her mouth, " 'the guilty flee when no man pursueth.' "

Stacy glanced at her mother, at the cool, gray eyes, the unruffled face, the straight figure, and unconsciously her own back stiffened, her head lifted. She followed her mother, and Harriet and Caroline brought up the rear.

The room was filled with little knots of people standing around, buzzing. Caroline slipped off to join Eunice Gailord, and Angela and Elena Ketchum and Harriet joined a largish group. None of Stacy's friends were present. Listening to the conversations around her, she could hear no reference to the sermon. One group was discussing a dinner party, another, the pros and cons of feeding the starving Peruvians since their own ruling class wouldn't feed them, and a third, what was wrong with Evie's bidding. The maid, June, threaded her way through the groups with a tray of pastries. "Good morning," Stacy said, and then she wondered if it was her imagination or if June's eyes had flickered with something—curiosity?—before she had answered, "Good morning, miss."

"Great weather. It's a sin to be cooped up here on a day like this." Stacy turned and saw Andy Newhouse. She tried to think of something to say but all she could think of in connection with Andy was one, that he was crazy about her, and two, that he had joined the army after college to avoid joining his father's brokerage firm. It didn't seem feasible to ask, "Are you still carrying a torch for me?" or "Getting along any better with your father these days?"

"Then why are you here?" she asked, and realized that was wrong too. His answer was a wide grin.

Behind her, Angela was saying, "Harriet, you weren't listening to Dr. Trowbridge," and Harriet answered, "But Angela, it's common knowledge. I wouldn't mention it if everyone didn't know about it anyway."

Irrelevantly Elena said, "Now, Harriet, bread cast upon the water—"

"Gets soggy," said Andy, and Stacy, who had almost forgotten him, laughed. But her attention wandered back to the conversation.

"I've been all over the country," Andy said, "and I never saw a drearier-looking group. Why is it, with a higher per capita income than practically any other congregation in the country, they have to go out of their way to look so damned humdrum?"

Stacy giggled guiltily. "Now, Andy, bread cast upon the water—"

Plaintively Harriet was saying, "Well, I *thought* you knew. Practically everybody knows that the Newhouses have a relative—Pat's mother—in an insane asylum."

Stacy, prone to blush anyway, turned a deeper red than usual. She felt like burying her face in her hands, but soothingly Andy said, "Don't feel embarrassed. God knows, we never tried to keep it a secret."

"Why, of course not—I mean, it's no disgrace—"

"Yes, it happens in the best families." He grinned.

Helplessly she grinned back. "People," she said. "They're awful."

"It just so happens I'm working on something better."

Again they grinned foolishly at one another like children, and Stacy was feeling much better when she heard something else, this time from a smaller group on her other side. It was a man she didn't know. "That's what I understand from the police. They're keeping it quiet, so don't spread it around, but I happen to know this Sergeant Murphy pretty well—he chases our horse every time he runs off and I always slip him something. Anyway, he said that Mrs. MacLeod got to the upstairs landing that

69

night and happened to look out of the window. That was before she found her son so she didn't think too much about it at the moment. But she saw a figure running down the road. She swears it was a woman, tallish and wearing a light coat and scarf. It isn't much—all the women around here are tall—but it's something. Talking about Sergeant Murphy, he's the funniest—''

Stacy didn't wait for the rest. Muttering something indistinguishable to Andy, she walked away to round up her family.

IX

Healey Mockridge hung up. "I'll be damned."

"Probably," Kitty said. They were in an alcove of the kitchen having a Sunday brunch. "You wouldn't let me go to church this morning."

"This woman said, 'Ask your wife what happened when she was in boarding school!' "

Kitty didn't move, but she couldn't control her face and it became puckered and spotted-looking. Whenever she needed time or was confused, she tended to repeat. " 'Ask your wife what happened when she was in boarding school'?"

"Well?"

"Well what?"

"What *did* happen when you were in boarding school?"

"Once I sneaked cigarettes into my room."

He looked at her sharply. "Why should some kook telephone to say a thing like that?"

"Because she's a kook. Did I tell you Stacy called yesterday—"

"Speaking of kooks?"

"—and said Will is going to their house for dinner tonight and we're invited too?"

"What's making you so supremely disinterested in that call? It's almost as though you *do* have something on your conscience."

"Oh Healey, it's probably some silly kid—"

"It was a woman. I told you."

"Then it was a disturbed woman. Ever since Johnny MacLeod was killed, more disturbed creatures have been crawling out of the woodwork—"

"Now what made you bring up Johnny MacLeod?"

"What? Oh—I don't—yes, I do. I read somewhere that when President Kennedy was assassinated, there was an increase in manifestations of mental disturbances throughout the country. Now, in a smaller way, this ugly event in Highlands has brought out—"

"Oh spare me."

"Very well, I will. I have to go to Mavis' anyway."

"Mavis'! For Christ sake, Kitty—"

"That's what I'm going for."

"—why must you always be— What does *that* mean?"

"We're planning the church supper and you just said—"

"You know something? There's an increase in mental disturbance in *you*. And come to think of it, it started with Johnny's murder."

"I'll see you later." She leaned over to kiss him lightly, but he grabbed her and bent her backwards in a theatrical version of a passionate embrace. In a moment it became less of a parody and more of the real thing. Disengaging herself breathlessly, she said, "Listen, Mavis is waiting—"

"She'll have to get in line. I can't handle more than one at a—"

"I promised. I can't simply—"

He let her go so abruptly she nearly fell. "We never have time to talk anymore."

"Oh? Is that what you had in mind?"

"Among other things. You're always busier than a one-armed paper hanger. And this evening we're going over to Stacy's. In the winter you're always correcting papers—I think you ought to quit teaching."

"What would I do with myself all day?"

"I'll go to work late and be home early. I'll find *something* for you to do."

"What a good game you talk. I'll be back shortly."

"Maybe if you'd stop working, you'd get pregnant." He looked at her sharply again. "*Now* what's wrong?"

She began clearing the table. Without looking up, she asked, "Healey, suppose we never have children? Will you—I mean, would it mean a terrible lot to you?"

"A terrible lot. Jesus."

"That reminds me. I've got to run." She stacked the dishes and, without changing her cotton slacks, went out to the garage.

All through the meeting she remained absent-minded and preoccupied. It was only when she heard Harriet's name mentioned that her mind came into focus.

"—asked for Mrs. MacLeod so I told him."

"How did you know it wasn't someone who wanted to kill *her* too?"

"Oh, come on."

"What's this all about?" Kitty asked.

"What's what all about?"

"What you were just saying."

"Kitty, where've you been?"

"I'm sorry. My attention wandered."

The others exchanged glances. "Kitty girl, you are *enceinte* or something?"

73

"No, I'm not *enceinte* or *any*thing," she answered shortly. "What are you all talking about?"

"Well, when I drove into town this morning to get the newspaper, I passed the MacLeod house, and I saw this man just leaving. I knew Harriet wasn't home and I stopped the car and got out—"

"Weren't you nervous?"

"Nervous! Why should I be? It was daylight, and just because *one* person was killed in the house—"

"All right. Go on."

"Well, I asked if I could help him. He said he was an acquaintance of Johnny's and had heard the news, and since he was in the area anyway, he wanted to drop in and offer his sympathy to Mrs. MacLeod. So I told him she was staying at the Huberts'."

"Oh," Kitty said slowly, as though examining the information. "What was his name?"

"How should I know? I didn't ask for his credentials."

"What did you say about killing her too?"

"What? Oh that. Mavis said I shouldn't have told a stranger where Mrs. MacLeod was. He might want to kill her too."

"Why?"

"Heavens, Kitty. It was a joke. Are you all right?"

"Funny you should ask. Healey and I were discussing that this morning. We were saying the whole town has gone to pieces since Johnny was killed."

"You mean because we all loved him so?" Mavis asked in astonishment.

Cautiously Kitty said, "Uh—not exactly. I mean that an act of violence often engenders more violence—" Having successfully shifted their attention from the particular to the general, Kitty fell silent. When the meeting was over, she hurried home to change.

As they drove up to the Hubert house later that afternoon,

74

they saw Stacy and Will sitting on one of the side terraces, having their drinks. Stacy was wearing a wildly printed shift that paled the end-of-the-summer zinnias and phlox behind her. The flowers, unlike Stacy, were frowzy and overgrown, like questionable crashers at a well-behaved party.

"Hi, you all," Stacy said, getting up. "We'd better go in and be sociable." Stacy was visibly ill-at-ease about something and Healey noticed it immediately. As they walked past the French doors to the drawing room, he said, "Stacy, you and Kitty are coming apart at the seams. What's wrong?"

Stacy flicked an invisible insect off her cheek. "Me? Kitty? You're imagining it."

"—damage from nature is never as bad as the damage done by man himself," Angela was saying to a group composed of Harriet, Frank and a man who looked vaguely familiar to Kitty. The newcomer was a tallish, dark man with a face so narrow and sunburned it seemed almost desiccated.

Angela made the introductions. The stranger was Joseph Ritacco, the friend of Johnny's who had been at Stacy's engagement party. He had found out where Harriet was staying through some fortunate accident (Angela was vague on the point, but Kitty could have explained it to her) and Angela had invited him to dinner.

Conversation lagged as Frank dispensed drinks. When he freshened Stacy's, a familiar expression crossed his face, one he was hardly aware of: an expression of almost wistful wonder at having produced all this loveliness. He put his arm around her shoulders and she looked at him, puzzled. There was something about him that reminded her of an animal sensing danger to its young.

"Thank you for a lovely time," Caroline shouted at someone outdoors, and then there was the sound of a car door slamming and a motor starting up. Caroline, wearing jeans and a turtle-neck shirt, came bounding in. "Hello, everybody."

75

"Caroline," Stacy said impatiently, "don't—I mean, you're so *much*."

"And I love you too."

"Hurry and change," Angela said. "We're having dinner shortly."

"Do I have to? Can't I have a sandwich in the kitchen with Gwen?"

"This is my daughter Caroline," Angela said to Ritacco. "Caroline, Mr. Ritacco."

Caroline approached to shake hands and Ritacco said, "She doesn't have to change on my account."

Angela opened her eyes faintly, but she didn't answer. Instead she glanced at Caroline, who bounded off in the direction of the stairs. As they were settling down with their drinks, another car door sounded.

"My, it's gay around here," Kitty said dismally. Expecting an interruption, no one made an effort to begin a conversation. In a moment Gwen entered. "Mrs. MacLeod—" But before she could say anything further, the visitors were in the room, two men, both large and middle-aged. "Sorry to disturb you, Mrs. Hubert," one said. "We—"

"They said they wanted to talk to Mrs. MacLeod," Gwen explained.

"We thought that since we were here, we could save time by talking to everyone at once."

"Pardon me?" Angela said. She was standing, her eyes cool.

The man who was doing the talking held out his wallet and Angela looked down. The card explained that he was Detective Thomas Holmes of the town of Summit which included Highlands. "We're from the police, Mrs. Hubert. We told Mrs. MacLeod to keep in touch with us and she told us she'd be here for a few weeks—" He stopped as Angela winced. "Is something the matter, Mrs. Hubert?"

"No—nothing."

76

"—and since we wanted to ask her something, we thought maybe we'd talk to you too. We'd like to see everybody who knew Johnny MacLeod."

"Well—we were just about to have dinner—"

"It won't take long, Mrs. Hubert."

"In that case, won't you sit down, Mr. Holmes, and uh—" She glanced at the other man, but he neither volunteered his name nor sat down.

"First, Mrs. MacLeod," Holmes said, "is this your earring?" He held out something and Harriet rose eagerly. Grabbing it, she said, "Yes! Where did you get it? Do you know who killed Johnny?"

"No, I'm sorry, Mrs. MacLeod. Some kid found it on the road. It was just outside your house, hidden in the grass."

"Oh." Disappointed, she sat down again. "Right in front of my house."

"Yes."

"Does it have any fingerprints on it?"

"It would be impossible to find fingerprints on something like that, Mrs. MacLeod. It's small and rough-surfaced." With no change of expression he added, "Miss Hubert, do you chew gum?" But he made a mistake and looked at Kitty.

Slowly Stacy said, "*I'm* Stacy Hubert. Yes, I do chew gum. Why?"

He turned to her and blinked. "May I ask what kind?"

The detective who was standing moved unobtrusively so that he was equally distant between the French and the front doors.

"May I ask what kind?" Holmes repeated.

"Pepsin. Why?"

"We found this near Johnny's bed the night he was killed."

He held out his palm. Not looking at anyone else in the room, Stacy reached out and took the object he was holding. It was a balled-up scrap of paper and foil. She started to unwrap it and then looked up inquiringly. He nodded and she continued what she was doing. "A pepsin wrapper," she said.

"Can you account for its being found in Johnny MacLeod's room? I mean," he continued smoothly, "were you in Johnny's room earlier that day and could you have dropped it then?"

She stared at him fixedly for a moment, and then, surprisingly, she smiled. Like Ritacco, he was misled by the wide blue eyes. "I was *never* in Johnny MacLeod's bedroom. Either that night or earlier in the day."

"Then how do you account for your gum wrapper being there?"

Her smile widened. "*My* gum wrapper wasn't there."

"You mean somebody tried to throw suspicion on you?"

"Mr. uh Holmes? Yes, Holmes. Surely it has occurred to you that other people chew pepsin gum."

"Not in this town," Harriet said quickly and then added, "I mean, that I know of. Of course, I'm sure that wrapper isn't yours, Stace. Maybe somebody wanted to frame you." She looked around as though expecting to find that somebody in the room.

"Did *you* have any idea why Johnny MacLeod should be killed?" the detective asked Frank suddenly.

"Me? No, of course not."

"Does anyone have any ideas?"

No one answered. Will began drumming the table with his glass.

Hesitating, Holmes said, "There's been some talk that he was killed because he had something on the murderer."

Loudly and clearly Kitty said, "You mean he was a blackmailer?"

Harriet started to speak but the detective held up his hand. "Have you any reason for saying that—uh—I don't think I got your name."

"No, I have no reason for saying it. *You* said it."

"What did you say your name was?"

78

"Kitty Mockridge."

"I'm curious," Stacy said to the detective. "*Where* has there been some talk that he was killed because he 'had something' on the murderer?" Gently she dropped the inverted commas about the detective's expression.

"I'm afraid that's confidential," Holmes said pleasantly.

"Surely, *Mrs. MacLeod* didn't suggest that her own son was a blackmailer?" Stacy asked, just as pleasantly.

Three people spoke at once. "That's not what I said," the detective objected.

"I resent—" Harriet began.

"Stacy, stop it," Angela said. "Is there anything further you'd like to ask us, Mr. Holmes? I'm afraid our dinner may be overdue."

"Is there anything someone can tell us? Something you saw or heard—"

"I thought it was burglary," Healey said suddenly.

"Well, that's what the murderer *wanted* us to think. But why would a burglar pick the MacLeod house? No offense, ma'am, it's just that there are bigger and fancier—"

"Well, the house *is* right in town. And if it was a kid, he wouldn't have a car. And if he was local, he would know the MacLeods kept their doors unlocked—"

"It's *possible*, I guess." The detective stood up. "Thank you, Mrs. Hubert. I hope we didn't spoil your dinner." Angela walked them to the door. When she came back, Frank stood up and said, "Drink, anybody?"

"I'll have one," Healey said. He looked puzzled.

"You know, Joseph," Harriet said abruptly, "this is the driest spell we ever had. Several people have had to move because their wells went dry."

"And you should see the lawns," Healey said. "Straw. Plain old straw."

"My mother lost a whole line of trees," Will contributed.

"I've heard that this dry spell has done something to the water tables," Kitty said, "whatever *they* are. I mean, even if we *should* get a decent amount of rain, it will take five years to get back to where we were—water-wise, that is."

"It'll probably never rain again," Stacy predicted. "The world will simply dry out."

"Yes," Ritacco agreed. "Fire or ice, as the man said. I think he favored ice, destructive-wise, that is."

As the silence lengthened, Stacy and Kitty blushed and Healey and Will looked sheepish. Then the telephone rang, and in a moment Caroline shouted, "Mummy, can I go to the movies with Buzzy?"

"Buzzy who?" Frank shouted back and the tension eased.

"Oh, Dad," Caroline yelled with false irritation.

"Yes, you may," Angela said, "and if you have any further requests, come down here."

A door slammed upstairs and Ritacco said sourly, "What a nice normal American family."

Uncomfortably Will said, "We weren't being—that is, the weather has always been a sort—a sort of family joke."

"You two getting married soon?" Ritacco asked with intentional rudeness.

"What? Oh. Next spring."

"Impetuous," Ritacco muttered.

"We have to wait until Will can find a substitute for the office," Stacy explained hastily. "He can't simply leave all his patients for a month."

Gwen announced dinner and Will said, "Good. I'm afraid I have to leave early."

"Oh, Will," Stacy moaned, "not again." They trickled into the dining room and began helping themselves from a casserole on the sideboard.

"Sorry, buddy. Mrs. Carmody."

"There's always a Mrs. Carmody. I wish people'd stop having babies."

"If they do, we stop eating."

"We'll live on love."

"That's what Mrs. Carmody said to Mr. Carmody nine months ago," Healey said.

"You sure you never lived in Chicago?" Ritacco said impatiently to Frank. The conversation had obviously been annoying him.

Frank, who had almost forgotten his presence in his amusement at the same conversation, looked at him blankly.

"I can't help feeling I've seen you before," Ritacco persisted, not the least bit disconcerted by Frank's stare.

"Yes, Frank," Harriet babbled, "Joseph was telling me. He's sure he knew you—" The transfer of Frank's eyes from Ritacco to herself brought her up short. She didn't have the mettle of her son's friend.

"As President Arthur said to the nosy lady," began Caroline who had just entered and was helping herself to casserole, " 'Madame, I may be President, but my private life is my own' "—she glanced at Stacy and grinned—" 'blankety-blank business.' "

"Who's President Arthur?" Will asked. He held Angela's chair for her while Healey performed the same service for Stacy, and Frank for Kitty and Harriet. Ritacco had deliberately seated himself first.

"You don't know who President Arthur was?" Caroline asked in shocked tones. Then, as though he had just come to her attention, she added, "How come *you're* honoring us with your presence, Will?"

"Well, as a matter of fact, I *do* have to leave early so stop gabbing and sit down."

"Making babies again?"

81

"I don't *make* them, Fatso. I simply preside at their uh—
—debut."

"Let's talk about the weather again," said Ritacco. Then suddenly he slapped the table so hard the water glasses teetered. "I've got it!"

He looked around as though expecting someone to ask him what it was he had, but no one did. "I know who you remind me of, Mr. Hubert."

"Whom," Stacy corrected. "Which reminds *me*. Are you all boned up for the start of the new year, Kitty? I've been getting out my notes and brushing up so that the little dears don't get ahead of me."

It didn't stop Ritacco. "I was a cub reporter twenty-five years ago, and by luck I got in on a crime syndicate story. It was quite involved, with a murder and what not. You're the image of one of the men involved. What was his name? Give me a minute. I've got a great memory. Frank Colovito, that was it. Ever hear of him?"

"Isn't that interesting?" Harriet contributed. "Tell us more about him, Joseph. What did he do? Isn't it strange, he and Frank having the same first name."

"I guess that's what reminded you of him," Frank said. He got up to get the wine. "By the way, Harriet. I forgot to tell you. It's a surprise I cooked up for you. I knew you didn't want to be home alone, and I knew it must be uncomfortable for you here. I mean, staying all this time. Not that it's an imposition—" He stopped to pour himself a little wine and taste it. "Not bad. Where was I? Oh yes. Not that it's an imposition, but I know you'd feel happier at home, so I got you a maid for two weeks. She'll be at your house early tomorrow morning. Naturally, it's my treat."

X

When Kitty opened the door the following morning, she found Harriet MacLeod standing on the mat. She started to say, "Why, hello, Mrs. MacLeod, won't you—" and then she saw what Harriet was carrying: a scuffed, cardboard suitcase.

"Hello, dear," Harriet said, walking past Kitty into the small living room. She sighed and sat down. "I don't know what's wrong with me lately. Even walking to and from the car tires me out. It must be one of these new bugs the doctors invented."

"Would you like a cup of coffee, Mrs. MacLeod?"

"I've been nauseated all night. All that rich food at the Huberts—and the alcohol! Sherry before lunch, gin before dinner, wine at dinner, brandy afterwards. I don't like to sound critical, but it isn't a good idea to bring up children with such a poor example—"

Something in Kitty's expression made her break off. "Well, of course, I know people say Johnny drank, but they exaggerated. And if he did drink a little too much, it was because he got in with the wrong people. I think I would like a cup of tea, dear."

Kitty went to the kitchen, put on the kettle, and prepared a tray quickly. While the water heated, she went out to the living room again. Deciding that she could no longer ignore the suitcase, she said, "Are you on your way home, Mrs. MacLeod?"

"Well, that's what I wanted to talk to you about, dear. It's so awkward asking people for favors. But now that I have no one in the world— I don't want to burden you with my problems. You heard Frank last night. He practically told me I had to leave. I ought to be charitable—I suppose he may be worried about something, and that's what made him so rude—" She hesitated, as though hoping Kitty would volunteer something, but Kitty was silent. "Anyway, he made it impossible for me to stay."

"Has the maid arrived, Mrs. MacLeod?"

"Is the tea ready, dear?"

"We'll hear the whistle. I thought it was terribly generous of Mr. Hubert to make that gesture. Particularly after Mr. Ritacco was so annoying—"

"Joseph? How was he annoying? All he did was say that Frank looked like Frank Colovito. Why should Frank be annoyed? Unless he has something to hide. Did Stacy ever mention—"

"There's the kettle," Kitty said. In the kitchen she splashed the tea into the cup angrily and brought the tray back. "Did the maid arrive, Mrs. MacLeod?"

"Oh, her. I took one look at her and I knew she wouldn't do. Can you imagine? The first thing she did was ask me where the television set was. The second thing she did was tell me she expected two full days off a week—"

"But it's only for two weeks—"

"I couldn't stand it. Even free. I wonder if Frank would give me the money—it's all the same to him. Well anyway, I told her she could leave."

"You sent her away!"

"Yes, dear. And that leaves me all alone again."

"Would you like me to drive you to your cousin's house, Mrs. MacLeod?" Kitty asked, desperation creeping into her voice. "Oh, how stupid of me. You must have your car here."

"I can't go to my cousin's, dear. She went on a trip."

"A trip? When you just lost—I mean—"

"I know, dear, but she had planned it for a long time." Harriet hesitated, but Kitty was silent, and finally she had to do the whole thing herself. "I hate to impose. But I know you don't have all the help the Huberts have—daily cleaning women, laundresses, what not—and I could be a real help to you. I could wash dishes, iron—it would only be for a few days. Until my nerves settle down."

Looking down at her hands, Kitty found, to her surprise, that they were clenched. She loosened them slowly, watching the blood seep back into the white knuckles. "Of course, Mrs. MacLeod."

"How sweet you are, dear. I knew you'd invite a lonely old woman to stay with you. I've always been so fond of you and your parents. But I didn't want to impose on them, what with your father being sick." She got up. "Which room may I have, dear?"

Picking up the suitcase, Kitty led her to a tiny bedroom near her own. "It's not made up, Mrs. MacLeod. I'm afraid it's terribly small after the Huberts'—"

"How cozy it is, dear. I think the Hubert house is too cold. Everything perfect. Sometimes I have the feeling that it's nothing more than a stage setting. Do you ever get that feeling, Kitty?"

"I'd better do some marketing, Mrs. MacLeod. I wasn't prepared—that is, I'll need some things."

"Please don't go to any trouble on my account, Kitty. But if you have to market, anyway, go right ahead. I don't want you to feel you have to stay home and entertain me. Where are the linens, dear? If you could just show me—I'd like to lie down."

Silently Kitty went for linens, a pillow, blanket and towels. She made the bed while Harriet sat on a chair, fanning herself.

In the car she drummed the wheel with her fingers and said, "Damn, damn, damn," aloud. Finally she went to town, did some haphazard marketing and then, instead of heading home, drove to the Huberts. The front door was unlocked and she went straight in, calling Stacy. She finally found her on the back terrace with a large assortment of objects around her: an easel with the accompanying accouterments; a dictionary with Shaw's *Back to Methuselah*; a fashion magazine, and a guitar.

Kitty stared. Then she walked around wonderingly. "Are you sure it's enough? I mean, let's see, art, literature, music —will it keep you busy? Shouldn't you add some uh less 'fine' activity—like sewing?"

Stacy was happy to see her. Raising her arms in a theatrical gesture she said, "I don't know what it is—I'm looking for a meaning in life. I'm tired of this constant round of partying, drinking, bridging—tired, do you hear? I want to know—what does it all *mean*?" She put a hand to her head in mock anguish, but something went wrong with the gesture and she began to rub her forehead as though it hurt.

Dropping into a chair, Kitty said, "Mrs. MacLeod came to our house today. How does that go? Little Orphant Annie came to our house today—"

"She did what?"

"She fired the woman your father sent over and told me she was afraid to stay alone and could she move in with us."

Stacy didn't say anything. Moodily she kicked *Back to Methuselah*.

"Stacy, what does she *really* want?"

"What do you mean?"

"Honestly, you and I used to be able to talk, but lately—well, you've got some kind of a wall around you."

"Me? A wall?"

"You act almost suspicious."

"Suspicious?"

"Will you stop repeating everything I say? It's as though you don't trust me. And if you repeat, 'Don't trust you?' in that idiotic way, I'll throw this—this guitar at you."

"Don't throw the guitar. It's Will's." She began cleaning up the mess.

"Oh, God—if there was only someone I could talk to."

That did it. The despair in Kitty's voice made Stacy stop tidying and settle back. "Kitty, I trust you. I guess I have things on my mind I can't discuss with you. Just as you have something on your mind you can't discuss with me."

"Stace, some secrets aren't your own. My mother—"

"I don't understand."

"I think you do. My mother once made me give her my word not to tell anyone, but I have a feeling it's common property by now. Anyway, I'm sure Mrs. MacLeod came to my house to find out something. She wants revenge. She thinks if she can unearth some shameful secret, she'll have Johnny's murderer—"

"Then she *knew* Johnny was a blackmailer," Stacy said softly.

"Yes, how did you—I mean—"

Stacy's face was pale and again she began collecting brushes and paints.

Quickly Kitty went on. "I mean I once explained this to someone else—I think Mrs. MacLeod knew Johnny was a blackmailer but justified his activities some way—you know, by telling herself that he was doing them a favor keeping quiet. Someone else might simply have blabbed—besides, she couldn't stop Johnny if she wanted to. He was the type to walk out and leave her if she gave her any trouble. But evidently

Johnny never confided in her and she doesn't *know* what he had on anyone. So she's fishing. I mean, like those ridiculous remarks about your father—"

"What does she have on *you*, Kitty?"

Kitty was too wretched to fight. Tiredly she said, "I had an abortion when I was seventeen. Johnny found out about it."

After a while, when Stacy said nothing, Kitty looked at her. "Well," Kitty said, "aren't you at least going to repeat, 'You had an abortion!' or had you heard about it?"

As wretched as Kitty, Stacy said almost inaudibly, "You won't believe this—I'd almost forgotten. But there were hints—"

Kitty closed her eyes. "God."

"Why don't you tell Healey, Kitty?"

"How do you know I haven't?"

"If you had, why would you be so—I mean the worst that can happen is for Healey to find out. Isn't that right?"

"How well you know me. Stace, suppose *you* had done something—ugly—once. Something which could make Will leave you. Would you take a chance? Would you tell him?"

"But Healey's your husband, Kitty."

"And Will's your fiancé. So what? I don't think you know Healey too well. He's easy-going on the surface, but he can be awfully— What's the word I want? Rigid. Stuffy."

"Kitty, if *I* heard it, others will. You know this town. Tell him yourself before someone else does."

They were silent for a moment, and then, sighing, Kitty stood up and smoothed her slacks. "I'm a big girl now. I shouldn't come running to you the way I used to."

"Please tell him. It's tearing you apart."

An odd expression crossed Kitty's face as she stared at Stacy. She was on the point of saying something, but she changed her mind and lifted her hand in farewell instead.

In town she stopped again and went to the sweetshop to call

Healey. As soon as he came on, she said, "Will you take me out to dinner tonight?"

"Hell, no."

"Healey, please. It's important."

"What are we celebrating?"

"Nothing. It's just that—"

"My mother always taught me that nice girls don't call boys and ask for dates."

"We can't talk at home. We have a visitor, and I have to see you alone—"

"A visitor? Who?"

"I'll explain later. Meet me at—oh, *La Maisonnette* at seven." She hung up quickly before he could question her further and drove home.

She didn't know what made her go in quietly. Perhaps it was an instinctive caution now that there was a stranger in the house. It was the first time since they had been married that she and Healey had had a live-in guest.

Mrs. MacLeod's door was open, but Kitty didn't go in. Deciding that her visitor was probably in the bathroom, she stood still a moment examining the alterations that Harriet had made in the short time since she had arrived. The intended nursery had been furnished in the meantime with discards from Kitty's mother's house, but it had always been pleasant and colorful. Now, in the space of an hour or two, it seemed changed. For one thing it was already messy. There were crumpled tissues on the dressing table, books askew on the shelf, a scrap of paper on the floor, an open suitcase on the bed showing an unattractive display of yellowed underwear, stockings, a sweater, a pair of slacks, and a blouse, and the chest drawers stood open. Even the bed was at an odd angle as though Harriet had been searching for something.

How could the atmosphere of a room change in so short a time, she wondered. It was more than simple disorder. Something absolutely unpleasant had happened to the nursery and she shivered with superstitious fear. For one thing, it seemed colder. But that was nonsense, of course. Perhaps it was the contempt implicit in the way she had scattered her belongings. Perhaps it was Johnny's picture, in a cardboard frame, on the dressing table. Perhaps it was the stale smell of mold from the suitcase.

For some reason she cocked her head to listen and heard a whole battery of sounds—a car on the road, Harriet's clock ticking, the pump starting up. Then, making up her mind, she stepped into the room. Her hand made an odd motion as though she were brushing away cobwebs. Instantly Johnny's picture caught her attention again, and she wondered if there was something wrong with the face itself, or if she only thought so because she had known him. One thing was certain—she could never put any baby of hers in a room once occupied by Johnny MacLeod's mother. She would put the unconceived baby in the study.

It was then that she became aware of sounds previously submerged by the clock and the pump—the soft, scraping movements of someone trying to be quiet. They were coming from the study.

Her own footsteps muffled by the carpet, Kitty went down the hall. Harriet was in the tiny study, bent over one of the shelves. Kitty couldn't see what she was doing.

"May I help you, Mrs. MacLeod?"

With an exclamation of shock, Harriet dropped what she had been holding, and Kitty heard a muffled thud on the carpet, followed by the clink of one piece of metal hitting another. Without giving the older woman a chance to retrieve whatever it was, Kitty bent to get it.

"My goodness, dear, you startled me. Whatever possessed you to come in so quietly? Don't bother getting that. I can—"

90

Kitty stepped back as Harriet tried to take the object she had dropped. It was a twisted wire with two keys hanging from it, one gold color, the other silver. It looked familiar to Kitty.

"My keys," Harriet said breathlessly. "Thank you, dear."

"Isn't that odd? They look so— Let me see. Yes." Kitty inserted the silver key into the file cabinet lock, and instantly the cabinet opened. "You made a mistake, Mrs. MacLeod. They belong to us."

"Do you know what?" Harriet said ruefully. "I had my house keys out—I was examining them. I've been thinking of having the locks changed in our house, and then I came into this room to look for a book and I must have picked up the wrong keys—"

"Why would you change your house locks?"

"You know, dear, because of the—because of what happened to Johnny—"

"But no one used a key to get into your house. You told the police that you always leave your doors open."

"That's right. I just remembered. I've been so confused lately."

Examining the shelves Kitty said, "I don't see your house keys, Mrs. MacLeod."

"What, dear?"

"You just said that you came into this room looking for a book and that you had your house keys with you and you picked up the wrong keys, taking our cabinet keys by mistake. Well, where are your house keys?"

"Goodness, you sound like a detective, dear. You're confusing me. Maybe I didn't bring them in here. Maybe I left them in my room. You frightened me so when you sneaked in behind me."

"I see," Kitty said, looking at her steadily. Then she twirled the file cabinet keys and dropped them ostentatiously into her pants pocket. "I'm going out this evening, Mrs. MacLeod, but I'll prepare dinner for you before I leave."

"In the middle of the week, dear? Where are you going?"

Kitty's eyebrows went up. "Out, Mrs. MacLeod." Before leaving the room she carefully made sure the cabinet was locked.

XI

"Mrs. MacLeod is staying with *us*?" Healey asked incredulously.

Nervously Kitty glanced around the restaurant, wondering if anyone she knew was within earshot. "Don't shout. I can hear you."

"Who's shouting? Goddamn it, you're turning into a mouse lately. What's wrong with you?"

"Anyway, what could I do? She came to the door with a suitcase and practically told me she was staying."

"You must have encouraged her somehow—said something—"

"*No, I did not*. I may have said hello to her at the Huberts', but if that's being encouraging, we'd be knee-deep in house guests."

"I don't get it. We're about ninety years younger than she is and we've never been exactly pals with her—why you?"

Kitty twirled her drink, tried some and made a face. "It's like water. They never give you a decent drink."

"Since when are you an expert on decent drinks? And I asked you a question—why you?"

"I told you. I don't know."

"I wish she'd have come when I was home. I'd have told her, 'Sorry, no vacancies.' Or, 'Keep out. Quarantine.' "

"I doubt that."

"I'll be damned if she stays more than one night. Talk about in-laws. Imagine *me* having to put up with Johnny MacLeod's mother. I never could stand the son of a bitch."

"Why?"

"Why what?"

"Why couldn't you stand him?"

"He was a fairy, that's why."

"That's no reason."

"You know a better one?"

She looked around the dimly lit recesses of the restaurant again, seeing malignant eyes hidden in every corner. "Yes," she said so softly he didn't hear.

"Listen, is that why we had to eat out tonight? Because of Mrs. MacLeod?"

"It's lucky we did. Suppose you reacted this way in front of her?"

"Kitty, honestly, you've got to get rid of her. You don't know the problems I've got at the office. Pressures which would make you collapse. I can't have that woman pussyfooting around. She makes me nervous."

"I have pressures too. I'm going back to work soon—"

"Let's not confuse teaching kids how to add with what I go through. Gillon will be retiring before next—"

"Don't tell me you're eligible for *that* job!"

"Oh, God, what you don't know—no, dear, I'm not eligible for *that* job—"

"Don't call me 'dear.' It's Mrs. MacLeod's favorite word."

"—but there'll be a shakeup all up and down the line, which means I *will* be eligible for chief engineer of our division—"

"Oh, Healey, how glorious—"

"I don't have it yet. Also eligible will be Doug Cowan, Vance Beeghly—"

"Oh, you know Doug doesn't have your brains, and Vance—everyone knows how crude he is—"

"You know it and I know it, but does Orvis know it? And incidentally it won't hurt to be awfully nice to Elena and Merrill Ketchum for the next few months. How did I get off on this? Oh yes, so just get rid of your elderly pal because I'm going to be on edge."

"What do people have against elderly people?"

"Some of my best parents are elderly people. But I just don't like Mrs. MacLeod."

"Why?"

"You're full of inane questions this evening. Why? Because she's so damned—gooey, sticky—because she doesn't let her right hand know what her left hand is doing—because she reared a son like Johnny and then pretends she doesn't know about his little creature in the city—"

"You're so violent today."

"I told you, I'm on edge. Now *you* answer a question. Is that all you wanted to tell me?"

She looked at her hands and tightened them to keep them from trembling. She had tried to bring herself to this point many times before, and each time she had bungled it.

"Come on, Kitty, what's eating you?"

"The fox."

"What?"

"You know—the fox which was eating the Spartan boy—"

"On the phone you said, 'We can't talk at home.' What did you want to talk about?"

"I found Mrs. MacLeod poking through our file cabinet just now."

"Poking through our file cabinet? What in the world— How could she get the key? It's locked, isn't it?"

"She found the key on the shelf and I don't actually know if she had opened it yet, but there she was."

"Why should she be interested in our file cabinet? If she wants our canceled checks, I'll be glad to fix up a nice package—"

"She wants to find out something."

"Find out what?"

Reluctantly she lifted her eyes, searching for a mark of sympathy, but he simply looked baffled. The two years of marriage were stripped away, and he was the eligible, handsome Healey Mockridge again—a "wheel" and an athlete in college, a member of one of the "right" families in town, a white-haired boy in a big company.

"I don't know."

"Kitty, for Christ sake—"

"Stop yelling."

"I'll get up and shout at the top of my lungs if you don't stop saying that." Suddenly he grinned. "Remember the time Gee Gee Labrousse got up on a table at the club and said, 'Whoever thinks Wessy Rockmore is a teasing bitch, raise your hand.'?"

She looked at the grin and a great yearning overcame her. She wanted to be reassured. She wanted to be able to tell him everything and have him hold her in his arms and declare that it didn't matter. He would love her no matter what she had done or would do.

"Healey—Johnny MacLeod was blackmailing my father."

The smile faded slowly, as though it took some time for him to digest what she had said. The fear almost paralyzed her vocal cords, but now that she had started, she had to get it over with. The words tripping over one another, knocking each other down in their panic-stricken effort to escape, she said, "He was blackmailing my father because of me. He found out that I got pregnant and had an abortion when I was seventeen."

At first he didn't seem to have heard. Just as her processes had accelerated, his hand slowed to a standstill. Nothing happened. The waiter came to the table, smiled pleasantly and asked, "Are you ready to order now?"

The two of them looked at him like children who had stumbled into a foreign restaurant and couldn't understand the language. Healey, for some reason, started to get up, forgot where he intended going, and subsided. "Uh—no, not yet. Another round, please," he said indistinctly. The forced words loosened the bottleneck and when the waiter had left, he said, "Why didn't you ever tell me?"

"I was afraid," she said almost inaudibly. "I didn't want to lose you."

His face was puckered into tiny lines. Disoriented-looking, he didn't seem to know where he was or what he was doing. He picked up a matchbook and twisted the matches out, dropping them on the table one at a time.

"My innocent little Kitty," he said wonderingly.

"Please, Healey—"

"I even believed the story about the doctor. God, I was naïve."

"Healey, please. It was *I* who was naïve. I was so young and stupid—"

"Not all that stupid," he said. The machinery was oiling up, gliding along more smoothly. "Tell me, who was this beast who took advantage of you?"

She shut her eyes and told herself that she wasn't going to be sick, but she didn't know whether to make a run for it or fight it. Fight it, Healey always told her when they were out sailing. Nausea is all psychological. She took a sip of her drink.

"Funny," he was saying, "that's what I liked most about you. Your innocence. The others were too sophisticated. I got tired of the husky voices and the dirty words. Those girls —eighteen years older than time. But you were innocent." He came to a stop. Then, "Who was the lucky guy?"

97

"Healey—I have to go home."

"I asked you a question. I'm sorry to sound stuffy, but you will admit my right to know?"

"I don't feel well."

"Baby, I don't blame you. I wouldn't feel well in your shoes either. Or your pants, I should say."

She started to get up, but he caught her wrist and exerted enough pressure to make her sit down. "Who was he?"

"Why do you want to know?"

"So I can kill him, of course. Isn't that the right thing to do?"

"Healey, let go of me."

"Sit still." His voice was soft, but something in it made her stop struggling. "You're making a scene you know," he continued gently. "If we leave without eating, everyone will look at us. And that's what you dread most in the world, isn't it? Now tell me who it was."

He had released her wrist and she covered her face. Then, almost immediately, she put her hands in her lap and straightened her back. "You won't believe it. I don't even remember anymore. He was a roommate of Mal Haskell's. Mal brought him home for Christmas. There was a party—I forgot whose—"

"You seem to have forgotten a lot for so memorable an occasion—or wasn't it the first time?"

"—and the boys had whiskey in the car. I'd never had a drink before. Somebody gave me a paper cup full. And then in the car going home—all I can remember is how cold it was—I guess it was *because* I was so naïve—"

The waiter returned with the drinks and put them on the table, but neither one of them noticed.

"So that's why I'm having so much trouble having an heir," Healey said unexpectedly. And then, in spite of what he had told her about eating, he motioned to the surprised waiter, dropped a ten-dollar bill on the table and led her out.

They had come in separate cars. With elaborate courtesy he opened her door and waved her in. She felt as though she were suffocating. ''I hope you and Mrs. MacLeod will be very happy together.'' He laughed and turned back to his own car. With a grinding of gears he drove away.

XII

Elena, sitting alone in the living room checking names on a list, noticed lights on the road. She watched them a moment, and when they didn't move she got up to look. They were the parking lights of a car. She tried going back to her list, but when ten minutes had passed and the car still hadn't moved, she went to the telephone. Dialing a neighbor's number, she asked to speak to Merrill.

"Merrill, how much longer are you going to sit around gabbing with Wilkie?"

"Why? It isn't late."

"Well, I don't like to sound like a hounding wife—it's just that there's a car parked on the road in front of the house and it bothers me."

"It's probably kids necking."

"But why are the parking lights on?"

"Shows they're sensible. They don't want to get hit."

"If they're necking they ought to be on a secluded stretch of road, not next to our driveway."

"All right. Let me finish this drink."

100

She went to the hall which was dark and watched the road through the glass panel on the door. Worriedly she remembered that Valerie was out and would have to pass the car when she returned.

Headlights approached from the direction of the neighbor's house and she took a breath of relief. She stepped outdoors, although it was chilly, to hear what would happen. When Merrill's car stopped, the door of the parked car opened and the inside was illuminated. Instantly her fear revived. She saw three or four figures—all male—and one had his head tilted back as he drank from a can of beer. Two of the figures stepped out of the car.

"Merrill," she called from the doorway, "shall I telephone the police?"

It was Wilkie who answered—evidently Merrill had had the foresight to bring along reinforcements. "Stay there, Elena. We'll tell you if we want the police."

"You're parked on private property," she heard Merrill saying.

"It's a town road, mister." To Elena's surprise the voice did not sound uneducated.

"What are you doing here?"

"We're sitting."

"You're next to my property. Get going or my wife will call the police."

"Call them." The voice sounded familiar to Elena. It was like meeting a store clerk away from the store, knowing he looked familiar, but being unable to place him. "And when she gets the police," the voice continued, "she can tell them what Johnny MacLeod had on you."

Elena shrank back. She felt horrified at her own stupidity in calling Merrill. She knew to whom the voice belonged now. A local youngster, about sixteen years old, who had often run errands for Johnny. Not an unfamiliar "tough."

There was a laugh, the car door slammed, and the car, with a sudden lurch that almost sent Merrill spinning, roared off in the direction of the village.

Elena continued watching as Merrill turned his own car around to take Wilkie home. He was back in five minutes, angry and flustered. "What in hell makes you so nervous?" he demanded.

"You sounded pretty nervous yourself. After all, they were parked right in front, and Valerie will be home soon—"

"This will make a great story around town. Wilkie'll tell Ruth, and she'll tell the garden club crowd—"

"Who asked you to bring Wilkie?"

"You sounded so damned nervous. I thought it was the Mafia."

Elena sat down. "What's happening? Who's putting them up to all this?"

"It could be Harriet." He went to the bar, poured himself a drink and joined her. "Or it could be no one. They hear their parents talking—and they liked Johnny—this is their way —maybe—of trying to find out who killed him. Or they're just being kids. They want some excitement—"

The doorbell rang and they stared at one another. It was Elena who finally jumped up and turned on the outdoor lights. "Who the hell can that be?" Merrill asked, not going to the door. Peering at the lit terrace, Elena said, "Why, it's Harriet." She opened the door.

"What in the world is going on here?" Harriet asked, walking straight in. "Lights going on and off, both of you peering out of the window like scared rabbits—"

Bristling, Merrill said, "Some roughnecks were practicing early Hallowe'en tricks. We thought they'd come back." Elena said nothing. She was staring at the suitcase Harriet was carrying.

Abruptly Merrill said, "You know, Harriet, something funny

happened tonight. These characters parked in front of our driveway and shouted something like, 'Who killed Johnny MacLeod?' I hate to bring up a painful subject, but other people tell me the same thing has happened to them. I mean, somebody is filling their heads with nonsense. Do you have any idea who it is?''

Elena stared at him, admiring the direct tactics. It couldn't hurt since the story would get around anyway, and this way they might learn something.

Harriet, however, simply looked hurt. ''Me, Merrill? How should *I* know?''

''Well,'' he muttered, ''there are always unstable elements who—well, if they hear a lot of talk, it makes them act strangely.''

Dismissing the subject she said, ''I hope you don't mind my dropping in so late.''

''Why no,'' Elena said brightly. ''I'm working on the seating arrangements for the Chrysanthemum Ball—''

''I thought Angela was chairman this year.''

''She is. She asked me to do the seating. So we're just sitting around having a nice cozy evening— Would you uh like a drink?''

''No, thank you. My stomach's been bothering me lately. You know, the oddest thing happened at the Mockridges' last night.''

They both looked up expectantly.

''You know I was staying at the Mockridges'?''

''No.'' Elena wasn't sure why she lied about it.

''Well, you did know I was at the Huberts'. Frank practically told me I had to leave—''

''Frank did?'' Elena said in a noncommittal kind of voice. Merrill simply drank and waited.

''Frank was upset because Joseph Ritacco—Johnny's friend—told him he looked like a Chicago gangster. So he told

103

me to leave and I went to Kitty's. Something happened. They must have had a fight. Maybe I shouldn't tell you this, since Healey works for Merrill, but I guess everyone will know soon anyway, so I'm not really giving anything away."

"What happened?" Merrill asked, leaning forward.

"They went out to dinner. They didn't invite me to join them. I guess they wanted to be alone. I had an egg and went to bed early. I heard the car so I put on my robe and went out to be sociable. I didn't want them to think I was sulking because they hadn't invited me to join them."

"What happened?" Merrill asked impatiently.

"Kitty came in alone. I asked her where Healey was, but she was terribly rude. She said something about his having to go out again and then she went to her room. Then, early this morning—it was about six—Healey came home. I heard him because naturally I haven't been sleeping well lately—"

Elena nodded sympathetically, putting a restraining hand on Merrill, who was getting restless. She was as curious as he was but able to hide it better.

"—because of Johnny. So I got up to prepare his breakfast. I like to be useful when I'm visiting people. But do you know, he didn't even answer me when I said good morning? He packed a bag and he left." She paused dramatically.

"He could have been going on a business trip," Merrill said, but his voice was thoughtful.

"I doubt that. Where was he all night? Why didn't he speak to me or to Kitty? I think they've separated."

"Oh, I hope not," Elena said. "They're such nice people." She looked thoughtful, however, unconsciously glancing outdoors to see if Valerie was coming.

"And then, this evening, Kitty told me she was going to her mother's for a few days. She practically told me I had to leave."

Unable to control his eyes, Merrill glanced at the suitcase apprehensively. Like an inexpert swimmer trying to grab hold

104

of something, he said, "What was that you were telling us about Frank?"

"He couldn't have been more rude."

"That doesn't sound like Frank," Elena said reproachfully.

"Why was he rude?" Merrill persisted.

But Harriet wasn't giving too much away until she received payment. "Of course, this trouble between the Mockridges leaves me with no place to stay," she said ruefully.

Splashing around again, Merrill said, "Well, it's probably nothing. Lovers' quarrel. Elena and I fought like cats and dogs when we were first—"

"You're just trying to be nice about the Mockridges," Elena said, a little sharpness overlaying the gentleness. "But don't tear us down in the process. We always got along very well."

"You mean we never quarreled?" he asked teasingly.

"I don't ever remember your packing a suitcase, darling."

"I couldn't stand sleeping alone," he admitted. "I have cold feet."

Mollified, she smiled.

"I hate to go back to the house yet," Harriet said. "It's so big and lonely."

Her smile fading, Elena said, "Your cousin will probably be glad to have you."

"She's away," Harriet said, frowning with worry.

"I would suggest that you stay here, Harriet," Elena started, "but unfortunately—"

"Oh, Elena, dear, thank you!" Harriet said gratefully. "I knew you wouldn't let me down. Other people—they're nice when things are going well for you. But when you really need them, they disappear. You know how it is. I never thought Angela Hubert would throw me out. You don't know how I appreciate *your* kindness."

Blinking, Elena said, "Of course we're happy to have you, Harriet, but I do hope you won't mind the confusion. You know

105

Valerie always has mobs of friends here all the time"—which wasn't strictly true, but it sounded young and gay—"and, of course, with Denise living in, we're sort of filled up. I hope you won't be uncomfortable."

"Oh no, dear. I'll be fine. Put me anywhere. The study will do—" The Ketchums exchanged glances and Harriet waited, as though expecting an interruption, but when none was forthcoming, continued. "I can always sleep on the couch in there."

"No, that's all right. We have an extra bedroom upstairs." Then, noticing how that contradicted her previous statement, she went on, "But Merrill's mother and father will be arriving from Tulsa soon and we won't have the room—"

"It's funny," Harriet said humorously, "how many people in Highlands have out-of-town relatives coming to stay with them. Except the Huberts. Have you noticed? They have no one."

"What were you saying about Frank?" Merrill asked again.

"Well, I'm not really betraying a confidence. I see no reason not to tell you—"

Merrill and Elena leaned forward, the two of them looking oddly alike as they watched her. "We won't tell anyone," Elena promised.

Surprised, Harriet said, "I didn't tell you not to."

"Well, we don't like to gossip. And certainly I wouldn't gossip about the Huberts. Angela is closer than a sister to me."

"Is she? Well, I don't call what I'm doing gossiping. I call it investigating. I don't mind if anyone knows. I'd do anything, *anything*, to find out who killed Johnny." She waited for that to sink in, but the other two said nothing. Their eyes had become slightly glassy.

"Why do you suppose," Harriet continued, "that the Huberts never mention their background, their past—"

"Because there's nothing to mention. Their parents are dead and they were both only children."

"As I said, Joseph told me Frank reminded him of a Chicago gangster—"

"And someone once told me I reminded him of Winston Churchill," Merrill said.

"Joseph said it's uncanny—of course it was twenty-five years ago, but he said this man was the image of what Frank could have looked like twenty-five years ago."

"Who was the man?"

"A racketeer. It had something to do with the syndicates. Anyway he was mixed up in a killing and went to jail for a while."

"Oh, now really—" Elena said, but Merrill interrupted. "It ought to be easy enough to check. Your friend can go back and check the newspaper files."

"That's the trouble," Harriet admitted. "Suddenly Joseph backed out of it. I don't know if he became afraid or what. He said it was a mistake and he was sorry he mentioned it. He told me that, after all, the man had paid for his crime, and besides, he didn't really look much like Frank after all. And even if it was true, it wasn't right to crucify a man's family because of some mistake of the past."

"Did you tell the police?"

"Yes, but they pussyfoot. I think they're afraid of the Huberts. They say they can't just accuse Frank of being a racketeer. There's no evidence. And even if he *once* was, he isn't wanted for anything now—"

"They're right, you know."

"He may not be wanted by the police now, but I can see where he would kill Johnny if Johnny threatened to expose him. Look at the social position they have in Highlands. I know Johnny went to see Frank the same evening, before it happened."

The film covering Merrill's eyes seemed to become thicker. "Why?"

"Why did he go to see him? He told me he wanted to ask him something. He heard something odd about them and wanted to give them a chance to refute it."

"Did he tell you what he heard?"

"No."

"Why would he take it upon himself to go to the Huberts to 'refute' it as you say? I mean, why not simply ignore it?"

"So he could squelch the rumor if it was untrue," Harriet said promptly.

"I see." Merrill nodded several times.

"But Harriet," Elena said, "what do you hope to accomplish?"

"I want people to be aware of what's going on. If it's true, Stacy shouldn't be teaching, and Angela shouldn't be running the ball and serving on hospital committees."

"But what can *you* do?" Elena persisted.

"I can make the murderer nervous," Harriet said matter-of-factly.

They both stared at her and she went on. "If the murderer knows someone is after him—or her—he might get rattled. Make a mistake."

Rather belatedly Elena said, "Really, Harriet, you're talking about friends of ours. We're not going to be party to any plots against them."

"Look at it this way," Harriet said softly. "If the murderer is found, it would stop all the rumors going around about other people. You'd be surprised at the things people are saying. And there wouldn't be uh—telephone calls, and boys calling from cars." She looked at them innocently and they both seemed mesmerized by her eyes.

"I think if Kitty were less friendly with Stacy, and you, Elena, if you were less friendly with Angela, it would help bring on a crisis. You know, make them feel isolated—"

"I have no control over what Kitty does," Elena said, side-stepping the main issue.

"But Merrill is Healey's boss, isn't he?"

They were both silent at that, registering several things, but it didn't appear that shock had any part of it. A water tap dripped somewhere, a clock ticked and the maid went upstairs. Finally Elena said, "I still feel it's ridiculous."

"Another thing," Harriet said, as though she hadn't heard her. "I wrote out all my suspicions. Just in case."

"Harriet, what in the world—"

"Just in case someone tries to kill me."

XIII

She'd been teaching all day and needed the exercise. Although it was chilly, she wore only a loosely knit pullover and skirt as she walked briskly through the thinned-out woods behind the house. Fall had come early this year because of the drought, and it was easy plowing over the dead underbrush. Newer leaves, patched red and yellow as though by a colorful disease, covered the infinite layers beneath. Jelly Bean ran ahead, stopping now and then to cock his head. He heard a brittle crackle far off in the still air and took off like a shot. She tried to whistle him back but her only answer was a distant thrashing.

A cluster of black-eyed Susans were still growing in a sheltered copse and she bent to pick them for the cache pot in her room. Then she followed the sounds of thrashing and found Jelly Bean digging furiously at a not-yet frozen patch of ground. Uneasy, she whistled again, but he paid no attention.

She went over to pull him away and saw what he had—a thin gold ring with an old-fashioned setting that held an opal.

The flowers slipped from her nerveless fingers, joining the dead things on the floor of the woods. A wind whistled past the witch hazel trees, making her shiver. Finally she pushed Jelly

Bean away and dug quickly, bringing up the rest of it—a gold charm bracelet, earrings with tiny diamonds and sapphires, a string of small pearls.

She looked around as though expecting the woods to be filled with prying eyes. Everything was deserted. She carried the jewelry in both fists since she had no pockets and walked back to the house. At the edge of the lawn she stopped to make sure no one was watching. Then she ran to the French doors, slipped through the drawing room and went upstairs. She had just made her own room when Caroline, not waiting to knock, slammed in.

"Stacy, are you— What's that?"

"Caroline!" Stacy's voice was a shout. "Can't I have any privacy at all?"

"Well, gee whiz, all I—"

"Get out. Will you please get out?"

"What are you hiding?"

"Did you hear me? I said get out."

"You're the biggest pill lately. Nobody can talk to you. If that's what getting married does to a pers—"

Losing control, Stacy grabbed her by the shoulder and pushed her out of the room, slamming the door. Then she leaned back on it, her eyes shut. "Oh, Lord," she whispered. "Oh, Lord."

Five or six minutes passed before she could summon enough energy to get a handkerchief, wrap the jewelry in it and drop it into her handbag. She ran a brush through her hair and went out into the hallway.

Instantly Caroline popped out of her own room. "If you're going to town, I want—"

"No."

"Why not? There's nothing to do. I finished my homework."

"I'm not taking you anywhere and that's final."

"Honestly I think you must be going through change of life or something. I need hair spray."

111

"I'll buy it for you."

"But I want to go out—"

Stacy brushed past her and Caroline retreated, nearly tripping. Once she was on the road, however, Stacy's nervous energy evaporated and she looked exhausted. She drove slowly, her eyes turning from left to right, searching. Feeling in her purse, she found a stick of gum and began to chew.

Suddenly her driving became more purposeful. She swung the car around and went back, away from the village. The country became more rural, with longer distances between houses, and barns which were used as barns and not as something else. On her right a small herd of cattle grazed in the waning light, and on her left an iron fence stretched endlessly, marking an estate. The fragrance of hay drifted in through the open window.

Finally she came to a bend, and on a deserted stretch of road which disappeared beyond a second bend she found what she was looking for. To a stranger the white guard rail might appear to be enclosing a meadow ringed by a tangle of growth. But Stacy knew what it really was. She parked the car at the side of the road and got out, taking her purse with her. Oddly fascinated, she stood at the edge of the "meadow" near one of the posts and watched the weed-clogged water. Then, shuddering, she bent down and picked up a stone. Glancing up and down the forsaken road, she threw the stone with all her strength at the oozing mud. As she watched, the stone, with a sucking sound, sank beneath the surface.

She reached into the purse and took the jewelry out, stuffing the handkerchief back. Walking to a point where the mud seemed thinner, she glanced around again and threw the ring. It hung on a leaf and she moaned softly, her hand over her mouth, but then, like the rock, it gave up and slid into the thick pond. Her breath came in soft little gasps as, in succession, she threw

112

in the bracelet, the earrings and the pearls. Then, not waiting to see what would happen, she ran back to the car.

At that moment she heard a motor.

Again she moaned and stepped on the gas. The car stalled and then roared on the second try. Almost tearing the shifting apparatus loose, she put it into reverse, backed out, spun the wheel and swung around, dangerously close to the overgrown pond. Racing the motor, she put the car back into first and turned towards home, praying that the approaching car held no one she knew.

Before she could completely straighten out, however, a familiar voice shouted, "Stacy—Stacy, wait!"

XIV

Stacy had read about an escape once in which the hero had had to climb a sheer wall with the aid of spur-of-the-moment climbing equipment fashioned out of an iron bedstead and a window sash. Failing meant being tortured to death. All she was doing was standing on a deserted road at dusk in Highlands, and if she failed, it would only mean embarrassment. Nothing could be proved. But she was paralyzed, unable to make the slightest effort to extricate herself.

Will parked his car on the side of the road, came out and folded his hands companionably on the door of the wagon. *"Now what are you doing?"*

"What do you mean—*now* what am I doing? What else have I been doing?"

"Well, it just so happens that I have a list here. I'll start at the top. One, acting very irritable lately."

"That's because I never see you enough." She was beginning to relax, and she could feel the blood pumping through her veins with added acceleration, an effect Will always produced in her.

"Two, being the owner of a very sexy little—"

"While we're at it, what are *you* doing here?"

"You're right. The best defense is offense. And speaking of being offensive, I just met Healey at the drugstore and he didn't even say hello." Without warning he poked his head inside the car and kissed her. Then, working up enthusiasm, he opened the door, pushed in beside her and began kissing her more thoroughly.

"Where were we?" Stacy asked breathlessly after a moment. "Oh yes—what are *you* doing here?"

"If I were you, I'd try to becloud the issue, not clarify—"

He broke off as a car came around the bend, slowed up considerably at the unexpected sight of the two parked cars, and then almost stopped as the owner craned to see what they were doing. It was no one they knew, and Will stared back until the car drove off. When it was gone, he continued as though there had been no interruption. "Three, having a narrow puritanical attitude towards premarital—"

"If you're not going to tell me, we'd better stop obstructing traffic."

"Well, you know how irresistible Mrs. Martin is."

"Mrs. Martin?"

"The one who weighs a hundred and ninety pounds stripped, and has a wart in a place known only to her husband and to her doctor. I was at her house."

"Whatever for? Doctors don't make house calls anymore."

"Can't tell. Ethics. Your turn."

"I'm beginning to hate that word. It's a coverup for everything. I was at the dressmaker's. She's doing some altering for me."

"For God's sake, don't get altered."

"There's another car coming. We ought to—"

"Is this where your dressmaker does her altering?"

"This? Oh. Well, you see I thought I'd hit an animal. I

115

swerved and I almost got stuck on the side of the road. Then I got out to see if I had killed the poor little thing and I found out I hadn't."

He stared at her blankly and nodded his head several times, not in agreement with what she had said, but in response, apparently, to something he was thinking. "If that's your story, you stick to it."

"You know how much I love animals."

"I have about"—he glanced at his watch—"half an hour to spare for you. Let's go somewhere."

Stacy's misery had by now almost completely vanished. "I'm not dressed."

"For what I have in mind, you're overdressed."

"You think you're such a devil. I bet if I were more—amenable, you'd cut and run."

"Put me to the test. Head for the club. I'll follow."

As they walked into the clubhouse, something odd happened which disturbed Stacy more than she could have imagined a month before. Tim, the bartender, looking at them as they approached, said, "Good evening, Doctor," and that was all. Stacy said, "Good evening, Tim," but apparently he hadn't heard. They ordered their drinks and sat down. "Servants and salesgirls," Stacy said.

"What?"

"Servants and salesgirls. They're the weather vanes of society's winds."

"What in the world—"

"Hi there, you all." A couple they knew had come in and stopped at their table. As they chatted, Stacy examined them critically to see if she could detect a difference in their attitude towards her. I'm becoming paranoid, she told herself as she glanced around the room to see if anyone was staring at her. When her attention returned to the conversation, she heard Will saying, "A costume ball! I'm not going."

116

"Not go to the Chrysanthemum Ball? You've got to go."

"I'm too old to put on a sheet and wave my arms."

"Don't pay any attention to him," Stacy said. "He'll go."

"Well, if you say so, buddy. But no costume."

They discussed it awhile longer and then the other two left. As soon as they were gone, Stacy said, "Will, let's get married right away."

The words surprised Stacy as much as Will. She hadn't known she was going to say them until they were out. She sensed, rather than saw, Will slacken, as though he had let out his breath, and then he lifted his drink and nearly finished it. Finally he lit a cigarette. Behind Stacy there was a spurt of laughter as a family party came in.

"Why?" he asked finally.

"I—I don't know. I'm not even sure why I said it. It's just that—well, waiting for the spring seems so—unnecessary."

"You know I can't take off until I get that replacement."

"I mean, I realize you can't disappoint all those nice ladies who have transferred their affection to you during the term of their— But what I mean is, let's get married quietly and not go away until the spring."

"Your mother is planning a big wedding. It's all settled. Stacy, what's wrong? You've been as peculiar as hell lately. You act moody, and you don't look people in the eye, and you laugh at the wrong time—"

"It's this long engagement. It'll do it everytime." She smiled, but he wouldn't smile back.

"Why won't you tell me about it? If we're getting married, we ought to be able to tell one another anything."

"*If* we're getting married," Stacy repeated slowly.

"All I meant was if we're getting married immediately, which we're not. Oh, forget it."

She rolled the tablecloth up tightly to the edge of the table and then let it unroll again. It went badly after that. They didn't seem to have anything to say to one another and she refused a second drink. Finally it was time for him to leave and they parted at the door.

More miserable than before, she drove home slowly. She was almost at the door when she remembered Caroline's hair spray. Unable to face her sister's onslaught, she turned the car and headed back to town.

When she came out of the drugstore she saw Andy Newhouse buying a newspaper. His face changed like one of the traditional masks of the theater from tragedy to comedy as he said, "Been casting any bread upon the water lately?"

For a moment she was confused. The only thing occurring to her was the thought of the jewelry she had thrown out on the pond, and then she remembered their talk at church. "Hi, shouldn't you be back serving our country or something?"

"I don't know why nobody likes to see army men on vacation. Stockbrokers get vacations, store clerks, doctors, but not army men."

"It makes us feel insecure having you sit around instead of scanning the sky for enemy planes, or whatever it is you do."

"I'll scan some other time. How about a Coke?"

She didn't want a Coke, but she didn't want to go home either. "Sure. Love it," she said.

He took her arm and led her to the sweetshop. She glanced at him now and then, wondering why he seemed so young to her when he had actually been two or three years ahead of her in school. Perhaps it was because Will was over thirty.

"When's the wedding date?" he asked casually when they were seated.

"In the spring."

"Quite a long engagement," he said, staring moodily at an advertisement.

Annoyed, she said, "Not really. I'm not that old," and then she saw Mrs. MacLeod in the telephone booth.

"Chicago *Sun*?" Harriet was saying. "Give me the editor. How should I know which editor? I want a copy of an old newspaper. All right, connect me—"

At that moment Harriet turned and saw Stacy. She stared a moment, a number of expressions flitting across her face, and then she smiled uncertainly. Turning her back, she pressed against the door of the booth, shutting it tightly. Stacy could hear nothing else.

XV

The strains of Saint-Saëns' *Danse Macabre* emerging from the clubhouse caused Elena's stomach to lurch—a reaction she always had to a large party. She had been looking forward to it, but that didn't diminish her nervousness.

Merrill had difficulty maneuvering because the theme of the ball was "Come as Someone You Would Least Like to Be," and he was wearing a donkey costume—to indicate a Democrat. In addition, a light rain had made the grounds muddy, and he swore as his foot sank into a puddle. His other cause for annoyance was Harriet, who had seemed unaccountably anxious to attend. Trudging along on the other side of him, she was wearing the easiest costume she could assemble to indicate either a corpse or a ghost. (It was one of her own sheets because Elena, who enjoyed receiving gratitude without committing the act necessary to earn it, had, at first, offered a sheet, and when her offer had been accepted, had discovered she couldn't possibly spare one.) She reminded Merrill more of a spider, checking the web to see which creatures had become entangled.

The main ballroom was dimly lit and, in spite of the open

120

doors, filled with smoke. The combined noise produced by the guests and the band preceded the party by half a mile. Inside, the dancers resembled characters from a Kafka novel. Every kind of depravity or unfortunate condition was suggested, ranging from slavery and poverty to a woman who wore political buttons to indicate she was the wife of the current President. Those whose costumes weren't self-evident were continuously explaining them—Uriah Heep, for example, and Van Gogh; the latter had to keep his disabled side towards people to make sure they got the point.

Aside from the noise, conversation was difficult because the masks hid the revelers' identities. It seemed to the Ketchums that the drinks they had had before leaving the house weren't strong enough any longer, and they drifted to the bar. There they struck up a conversation with two Russians and after a while they began to dance. A man representing a Negro cut in on Elena because, as he explained, he believed in segregation, and she too was wearing black face. The noise and confusion grew, and as the air got closer, several people pushed aside their masks and Elena recognized Kitty's parents, the Brainards, and Dr. Trowbridge, the minister, who had come as the devil, as a matter of course. She invited them and another couple to join Merrill and herself at a table as far removed from the band as possible.

"What's Kitty wearing?" Elena asked as soon as they had settled themselves and ordered drinks.

"She isn't here," her father said shortly.

"Not here! But she's never—"

"She doesn't like costume parties," explained Mrs. Brainard, who evidently didn't either. Her costume consisted of a set of gardening tools.

The conversation broke into segments, and when she was sure she couldn't be overheard, Elena said in a conspiratorial voice to Mrs. Brainard, "Did Harriet talk to Kitty?"

The other woman leaned back a little as though to get a better view of Elena's face. There was nothing impolite in her voice, but she conveyed a distaste for conspiracies as she said, "Why should she?"

A little less confident, Elena said, "Well—I shouldn't talk about it—but it's just that Harriet said she was going to."

"What about?"

"Well—" Elena glanced around and lowered her voice. "She wanted to know if Kitty was seeing much of Stacy these days."

Mrs. Brainard frowned, as though trying to puzzle something out. "Why should Harriet MacLeod want to know if Kitty was seeing Stacy?"

"Don't breath a word of this—" Elena waited for Mrs. Brainard to agree that she wouldn't breathe a word, but the latter simply stared, making Elena even more uncomfortable. To offset her lack of ease, she spoke with even more girlish emphasis. "Harriet said—mind you, I don't believe a word of this—but Harriet said that if people were less friendly with the Huberts"—Mrs. Brainard made a motion, and Elena waited, but she said nothing—"that is, if they sort of isolated them, one of them might crack. She sort of hinted—well, actually, she more than hinted—that Stacy knows a lot more about Johnny's murder than she's letting on. Well, I'm sure you've heard the rumors—"

"Yes, and I was wondering who was spreading them."

"It's Harriet," Elena said, missing the point.

"I can't understand why you're telling me this."

"Harriet came to us," Elena said, gaining confidence as she mentioned a field in which she felt superior, "because Healey works for Narco Electronics too, and she felt that if anything came out in the newspapers about Stacy being the uh—you know, well, all her friends would be muddied too—you know, by association. And if Healey's name was muddied, why, it might reflect discredit on Narco Electronics. And, of course,

122

Merrill's life is tied up with Narco.''

The other woman continued staring at Elena. She wet her lips but seemed at a loss for words. Just then Harriet joined them, sitting down with a sigh, and Mrs. Brainard rose. ''Will you excuse me? I've hardly danced at all.'' She pressed her husband's arm and the two of them melted into the crowd.

''What were you two whispering about?'' Harriet asked.

''We weren't exactly whispering. We were discussing furniture.''

Andy Newhouse, dressed as Mussolini, and a girl who was Joan of Arc with the stake tied to her back, danced by just then, and Elena who had her eye on Andy for Valerie, stopped them and asked them to sit down.

''Whee,'' Andy said, tugging on the pillow that inflated his stomach. ''Never again.''

Looking at him with glazed eyes, Harriet said, ''Yes. I don't know why I came.''

''I never saw it so crowded.''

''It isn't the people,'' the girl said. ''It's the costumes.''

''All I can think of,'' Harriet said desolately, ''is Johnny. His first Hallowe'en. He was six and he was supposed to be a devil—like Dr. Trowbridge—and the mask kept slipping and there were those innocent blue eyes and blond hair—I guess what reminded me was you, Andy. He looked a little like you.'' Almost to herself she added, ''They start off so— You want the world for them, and then what goes wrong? What could have gone wrong?''

Andy looked down at the table and tried to think of something to say. Lifting his eyes he saw that Harriet was watching Stacy Hubert as Marie Antoinette and Will Tobin with a doctor's bag dangling from his waist. Angela and Frank dressed (rather obscurely) as Eurydice and Orpheus, nearly tripped over Harriet's sheet as they danced by.

Sadly, and without any bitterness, Harriet said, ''It's hard to

123

think of so many young people dancing, enjoying themselves, while all the time Johnny is out there— Forgive me.''

Elena put her hand over Harriet's. Suddenly moist-eyed, she seemed overcome by the thought of babies everywhere, and what some of them became, some of them did, and some had done to them.

After a while Andy and his partner drifted away, Dr. Trowbridge went to find his wife, the other couple, the Pattersons, decided to dance, and Merrill asked a streetwalker to twist. Harriet and Elena were alone. People jostled the table, and the confusion and stuffiness increased. Elena began to feel resentful about being saddled with Harriet. She tried to catch somebody's eye, hoping to be asked to dance, but no one noticed her. She was considering the ladies room as an excuse for moving, when Harriet said abruptly, ''Elena, I—there's—I—''

Elena took a close look at her and started up. Harriet's habitually sallow complexion had turned a ghastly white. Almost as Elena watched, bubbles of sweat erupted on her forehead and her hand gripped the table. She tried to stand and then she doubled up, clutching her stomach. Before Elena could grab her, she pitched forward on the table, her face hitting the wood.

XVI

It was the passing Uriah Heep who got to Harriet first. Elena backed off. Heep pushed up his mask, turning into James Goewy, headmaster of the day school, and lifted Harriet's face. "Get a doctor, quick!"

Ashamed of her initial weakness, Elena settled back into her own image of herself. She ran to the bandstand, pushing characters from fact and fiction out of her way, and asked the leader if she could make an announcement. "What is it?" he asked. "I'll—"

Unceremoniously Elena pushed him aside too and grasped the microphone. "Your attention, please. Is there a doctor in the house?"

A burst of laughter filled the room.

Elena's voice became stern. "I'm perfectly serious. Harriet MacLeod has been taken ill."

At that a jumble of voices started up, and since there were close to a dozen doctors present, a few began threading their way towards the bandstand.

"Dr. Hayden," Elena said, taking the arm of the first to arrive, "this way." By that time, however, Harriet had been carried into the ladies room. When Elena started to follow, the doctor asked her to wait outside. In a moment James Goewy came out, looking faintly nauseated, and stationed himself at the door. He told a man dressed presumably as Oedipus to get Mavis Haines, who had been a nurse once.

Everyone milled around in front of the door, and Elena got caught up in the whirl and found herself yards from the scene of action. To compensate, she gathered as large a group as possible and began recounting exactly what had happened.

The door opened again and there was a surge forward, but only another doctor was allowed in. Oedipus ran off on another errand.

One of the club servants turned on the overhead lights and the room resembled a preview of purgatory, except that the assembled sinners appeared anxious to go forward.

"Was *she* stabbed too?"

"I don't know. Ask Elena Ketchum. She was with her."

Elena was now the center of a mob. Judiciously, and with her face set in a sad expression, she said, "No, there was no knife. I'm not sure what it was. I wouldn't want to say, of course, without the doctor's opinion, but I think it was poison. She was holding her stomach, like this."

"Maybe she was shot."

"We'd have heard it."

"No, we wouldn't. Not with the band going."

"Don't you think someone ought to guard the doors to see that no one leaves?"

"Too late. A dozen murderers could have gone in and out by now."

"It doesn't matter. We have the guest list."

"Why does it have to be someone on the guest list? It could have been anyone. The doors were open, and what with masks—"

126

"Listen. Aren't we jumping to conclusions? How do we know it wasn't a heart attack?"

There was a sudden silence, as though a natural death were the most unnatural thing in the world. Accusingly they looked at Elena who said, "No—if you'd seen her face. It was terrible—"

"People who are having heart attacks look terrible."

Oedipus came flying back, holding several things.

"What is it?"

"Limes—mustard, too, it looked like."

"What are they doing in there? Having franks and limeade?"

"That's not very funny."

"That proves it's poison!" Elena said triumphantly and then quickly modified her voice. "Aren't those antidotes?"

A siren sounded in the distance and quickly rose to a wail. The buzzing in the room increased to an unbearable pitch as two white-jacketed attendants cut a swath to the ladies room. In a moment they came out, bearing a stretcher, and everyone craned to see Harriet. She was inundated in blankets and sheets, however, and her face was nearly invisible.

"Is she dead?"

"I think so. I think her face was covered."

"If she were dead, why are they taking her to the hospital?"

Another siren interrupted the speculations and this time two local patrolmen appeared. One of them went to the loudspeaker and said, "Quiet down, everybody. Quiet, please. Nobody leaves. Everybody sit down. Somebody close the doors."

Instead of diminishing, the noise increased in volume. For the first time Elena felt a prick of alarm. The pleasurable excitement drained away, leaving the sick feeling in her stomach. She wished now that she hadn't made such a point of telling everyone of her proximity to Harriet.

As though to italicize her fears, the patrolman now said,

127

"Everyone who spoke to Mrs. MacLeod or saw her, come up here. Up here, please."

"Is she dead?" a man shouted.

"I said quiet, please. Where's the woman who was sitting with Mrs. MacLeod?" He bent to consult with a helpful guest. "Will Mrs. Ketchum come up here?"

Elena, no longer enjoying the stares, stepped forward. She felt almost faint with apprehension. "Here I am," she tried to say in a firm voice, but it came out a squeak.

Behind her someone said, "Let's get a drink."

"Don't be heartless."

"What's heartless about it? They drink at wakes don't they?" There was a muffled laugh, and desperately Elena wished she could have been one of those free to surge towards the bar. She looked around for Merrill but couldn't find him.

"Sit down," the patrolman told her. "They'll want a statement later, but just tell me what happened."

"A statement?"

"Don't worry about it, ma'am. Just tell me what happened."

"Well, there's nothing to tell really. We were chatting together—over there, at that table. She's our house guest. We're very old friends and she came to stay with us when the awful thing happened to her son. We didn't want her to stay alone tonight so we insisted—"

"Just tell us what happened tonight, ma'am."

"I was. If you're going to interrupt—"

"Just take it easy, Mrs. Ketchum. There's nothing to be upset about. You were sitting at the table, you said. Then what happened?"

There was another diversion at the door. More men came in, not in uniform, but with an unmistakable air of authority. They spoke to one of the self-appointed guards at the door and then approached Elena and the patrolman. Desperately Elena looked around again and saw Merrill at the bar. She couldn't believe her

128

eyes until she saw him lift a glass and start towards her, and then she was so grateful she was afraid she would cry.

"Mrs. Ketchum?" one of the newcomers said.

"Yes."

"I understand you were with Mrs. MacLeod when she had her—when it happened?"

Instinctively Elena found herself responding to his brisk, business-like manner. She no longer had a desire to ramble.

"Would you mind coming with me, please?"

"Where?" she asked, the alarm flaring.

"To one of the closed rooms. It's too noisy in here."

Elena got up and waited for Merrill, who handed her a drink. "May my husband come too?"

"Certainly." The Ketchums, the man who had been asking the questions and someone else with a pad and pencil filed into the club office.

"Now, Mrs. Ketchum," the speaker went on when Elena was seated, "I understand you were at a table with Mrs. MacLeod. Who else was with you?"

"Lots of people. The minister, Dr. Trowbridge—"

"Your husband was with you?"

"Oh yes. My husband, Harriet, me, the minister, the Brainards—they're uh friends of Harriet's—they've known her for a long time—"

"Yes. Who else?"

"Let's see. The Pattersons. And Andy Newhouse. I don't know the name of the girl with him. Lots of people. You know, people who stopped to chat. People kept passing the table, you know—on their way to the uh rest rooms and such. I couldn't recognize many of them because they were wearing masks. The tables were awfully close and there were so many—"

"I understand. Just mention those you recognized."

"Well—I saw Stacy Hubert and Will Tobin dancing—"

"Did they come to the table?"

"Not that I know of. But as I said, people wore masks—"

"But you recognized them. Did they come to the table?"

"I—well, I wasn't watching every minute. I don't know. We were close to the dance floor. Ringside, so to speak. With such odd clothes on, people's uh—movements were veiled." She began rubbing the blackface off her skin with a handkerchief, as though to indicate her proper place in society. "Let's see, I think the Haineses stopped to say hello. Please don't think I want to get anyone in trouble. I'm only trying to be cooperative and give you a clear picture of what happened."

"Yes, Mrs. Ketchum. That's what we're here for."

"As I understand it," said Merrill a little pompously, "my wife doesn't actually *have* to talk to you. She's doing it voluntarily."

The detective glanced at him and then away, without saying anything, and Merrill became faintly pink. "I'm simply making a point. I would like to know if Harriet MacLeod is dead, and if she is, what she died of."

"Who do you think would want to kill her?" the detective asked Elena.

"No one. I really can't think of a soul."

"You're a friend of hers. Do you think it could be the same one who killed her son?"

"I hate to offer an opinion."

"All right. Go on."

"There isn't anything else. I mean, she said something—"

"What?"

"I forget. Just sort of an exclamation and I looked at her. She looked ghastly. She tried to get up and—oh yes—she held her stomach—and then she fell across the table. That's all."

"Who else was at the table at the time?"

"Well—let me think. I know James Goewy got to her first. He lifted her head—"

"Was he at the table?"

"Well—uh no. It's so hard to remember. He was near us and got to her first."

"You must remember who was sitting there at the time."

"Uh, let me see—I think the Brainards had just gotten up to dance—the Pattersons too—"

"Then just you, your husband, the minister and Mrs. Mac-Leod were at the table?" He hesitated, glancing at the man with the pad who said, "Andy Newhouse and a girl."

"So there were, let's see, six at the table when it happened?"

"Well—not exactly. Merrill had gone to dance, and uh yes, I think Andy and the girl left."

"Then, just you, the minister and Mrs. MacLeod?"

"Wait—Dr. Trowbridge had just gotten up."

"Then just the two of you were at the table?"

"I uh guess so—of course they had all been there a moment before—"

"Did you see her drinking or eating anything?"

"I don't think she drank— Just, yes, a glass of water—I think I did see her drink water—"

"How soon before it happened did she drink the water?"

"Well—I really wasn't checking. I mean, there was so much going on. I'm afraid I can't remember every detail."

"All right, Mrs. Ketchum. Just leave your name and address and we'll be in touch with you."

"You mean I have to talk to you again?"

Suddenly he smiled. "Is it that bad?"

She smiled too. "No, not really."

When Elena and Merrill emerged from the office, a group immediately surrounded them. "What happened?"

"Nothing."

"What did he ask?"

"I'm not sure if it's confidential or not."

131

"Has anyone heard if Harriet is all right?"

"Nope. I think they're having the contents of her stomach analyzed."

"How could they do that without cutting out her stomach?"

"Really. She threw up. That's how."

"What did they say it was?"

"Arsenic, I think."

"No, carbolic acid."

"Neither one. Oxalic acid. It looks like Epsom salts."

"Epsom salts? Do you think Harriet took it herself, thinking it was Epsom salts?"

"Why should Harriet take Epsom salts?"

"How should I know? I don't even know what Epsom salts is. Are?"

"Where do you get it?"

"Epsom salts? In the drug—"

"No, you ass. Oxalic acid."

"You planning on doing away with someone?"

"It's best to be prepared."

"I heard that it's present in cleaning fluids."

"Cleaning fluids? Then it was an accident. Some idiot cleaned a glass with some fluid and left some—"

"Not that kind of cleaning fluid. Clothes cleaning fluid."

One of the doctors appeared from the direction of the outer door. "It's all right," he announced. "She'll live."

Elena tried to adjust her face to some semblance of joy. She hadn't realized how much she had counted on Harriet's death.

XVII

Stacy couldn't keep her mind on anything. Virginia, her brightest student, was reciting, and Stacy turned the pages without hearing a word. Her mind was a kaleidoscope of fragments —Harriet MacLeod's face as she had pitched forward on the table, Will's voice as he told her he was tied up all week, Elena's evasive eyes as she had refused a bridge invitation from Angela. . . .

"Miss Hubert," Virginia said.

Stacy's head jerked, as though she had been wakened from a nap, and the class laughed. But not Virginia. Concerned, she asked, "Are you tired, Miss Hubert?"

"No, of course not," Stacy said briskly, trying to clear her blurred vision. "What's the name of the cuckoo parasite"—the class laughed again—"which leaves its eggs in the nests of other bees and starves their larvae?"

Again Virginia lifted her hand, but Stacy called on Phyllis. Phyllis, however, had lifted her hand in the hope that she wouldn't be called but would still be given credit for knowing. She didn't.

"The Nomada," Virginia shouted.

"Virginia! Don't answer unless I ask you to. Which bee takes the Osmia as host, lays its eggs at the bottom of the food mass in the cell while the host lays its eggs on the surface and then the larvae attack and devour the Osmia?"

"How mean," Phyllis said, hoping to make up in sympathy what she lacked in information.

"Who knows?"

Virginia began to fidget.

"It's the Stellis," Hollis Murphy said, leaning on one elbow and scratching his desk indifferently so that no one would mistake him for an intellectual. "My mother said the Stellis reminded her of Mrs. MacLeod."

It was as though a little fluff of dust which had been moving stealthily across the floor had just grown enormous. Stacy looked around but no one seemed to care. Some faces were blank and trying to look bright (Phyllis), some bright and trying to look stupid (Hollis), and some bright and making no bones about it (Virginia).

The afternoon limped on, filled with a world of drones being driven from the hive to starve after fulfilling their mating function; the aristocratic queen bee being fed royal jelly while the others subsisted on bee bread; predatory hordes devouring the just born, the weak and the outdated, and as the lesson progressed, so did an image in Stacy's mind of a revolting mutation: a creature with the bee's sticky body and Harriet MacLeod's head. Evolution's replacement for man (better suited to the future as man had once been better suited than the dinosaur) was setting a hairy Johnny MacLeod at the bottom of a food mass provided by an almost extinct Frank, and the master of the earth (did he too suppose he was made in God's image?) was reaching up to devour an outdated Stacy.

"Miss Hubert!"

134

"Er—yes?"

"The bell rang."

"Class dismissed."

Stacy went home quickly, avoiding even Kitty, and entered the house through the library in order not to have to chat with Gwen. Her father was there, however, making a telephone call. He terminated the conversation somewhat abruptly as she entered and grinned. "Hi, baby. Have a hard day at the office?"

"Who were you talking to, Dad?"

"Boy, am I glad your class can't hear you. Whom."

"Whom?"

"Nobody important. You don't look right. What's wrong?"

"What's wrong, what's wrong. If people don't stop asking me what's wrong, I'll scream."

He was silent so long she turned to look at him and instantly felt contrite at the hurt expression on his face. (When she had been small, he could always remedy anything: "My doll broke, Daddy." "We'll buy another." "Linny was mean today, Daddy." "We can take you to Julie tomorrow.") She put her hand over the back of his and he covered it with his other one. Like children confined to the house with illness, the two of them stared at the dreary expanse of lawn. The gardener had overlooked a mound of leaves and they moved desolately, mourning the dead summer.

Caroline, dropped by the school bus, came in through the kitchen and they could hear her chatting with the day maid. After a time she came searching for more stimulating company. Even she, however, lacked her usual exuberance. "Hello, everybody. Let's make a fire and roast something."

Her father roused himself. "Sure. What will we roast?"

"I'll ask Gwen if she has popcorn or chestnuts or something." A little happier, she went out, shouting for Gwen.

Stacy, with no word of explanation to her father, went up to

135

her own room. There she shut the door and dialed Harriet MacLeod's house. She waited while the bell rang six times and then she hung up. For a moment she hesitated, biting her lip, and then she dialed the Ketchum number. When the maid answered, she said, "May I speak to Mrs. MacLeod, please?"

"Mrs. MacLeod is resting. She can't get out of bed. May I take a message, please?"

"No, I'll call back." She changed to slacks and a warm jacket and went down the back stairs. This time she encountered Gwen, but since Gwen never asked questions, there was no problem.

In town she turned unhesitatingly up Harriet's driveway and drove to the back so that no one passing could see her car. The kitchen door was locked, which surprised her since Harriet never locked her doors, but she went to a ground-level kitchen window, removed the screen without much trouble and opened the window.

Hesitating a moment, she listened to tiny feet scurrying somewhere behind the walls. A roach scuttled into the greasy dust under a cabinet. No wonder Harriet preferred other people's houses, she thought. Finally she started downstairs.

Nothing but electricity and heat had been added to the basement since the house had been built some two hundred years before, and the weak bulb shed a dim light on the filthy dungeon. She went down quickly, each step requiring immense will power. The shadowy shapes resolved themselves into broken bedposts, torn mattresses, three-legged chairs, newspapers stacked so high they might have been accumulating since the house had been built.

Something brushed her face and she wiped off the clinging web with a handkerchief, making sure that nothing dropped from her pocket. She made a great deal of noise to warn off the mice. Finally, taking a deep breath, she took a rocker off the nearest trunk and began with that. Immediately she was assailed by a strong odor of moldiness. She put her hand in and began pulling out moth-eaten sweaters, hats, old dresses, jackets, coats and finally baby clothing. The last caught her attention, and examining the blue-edged christening dress, she tried to imagine Johnny MacLeod as a baby. It was impossible. Throwing everything back into the trunk, she continued her search. She began at the right of the stairs and worked her way around the perimeter, each time putting everything back.

She was completing her first circle and was back at the steps when she noticed that the dirt behind them didn't seem to be so thick. It then occurred to her that it was an accessible spot, easily reached from the stairs themselves. Sometimes Johnny must have wanted his material quickly. She pulled aside an ancient comforter and found cardboard cartons filled with papers. Eagerly she examined the first one and then she swore. They were Johnny's school notes—endless history, geometry, philosophy and language memorandums. Evidently nothing was discarded in the MacLeod house.

There were so many cartons and so many papers she began to feel discouraged. Taking one at random from each carton, she examined it and replaced it. Behind the cartons was a wooden spice chest, about two feet high, twenty inches wide and perhaps eighteen inches thick. The doors opened like a wardrobe and she pulled at them but they were locked.

Instantly her interest quickened. This was the first object she had encountered which someone had considered important enough to lock. She felt along the shelf behind the steps but couldn't find a key. Finally she tried lifting the chest. It was heavy, but she managed to get it up the stairs and into the kitchen.

Glancing at her watch, she put the chest on the table and went to the pantry where she knew Harriet kept her tools. There she found a hammer, and without hesitation she smashed at the ancient wood until it splintered.

Like a shipwrecked sailor who has been swimming for hours and finally feels the sand under his feet, Stacy took a deep, exhausted breath. At long last she had found Johnny MacLeod's blackmail file.

XVIII

Angela led Will to her bedroom, the only place in the house with an inside lock, and deliberately turned the key. "You look worried," she said, smiling. "I promise to act like a lady."

There was no answering smile on Will's face.

"Please sit down." Angela indicated the armchair and she herself took the chaise. It was turning dark and she switched on the table lamp. Instantly the Persian rug began to gleam like a jewel.

Angela didn't waste time. Lightly she said, "Stacy told me she proposed to you and you refused."

"There isn't much Stacy doesn't tell you, is there?"

"I suppose as present-day standards go, we have a pretty good relationship."

He glanced at his watch. "I'm afraid I don't have much time."

She looked at him so long and steadily, his eyes dropped. "You can always bill me for the visit," she said after a moment with slow, deliberate rudeness. "I thought I had the right, as your future mother-in-law—" She stopped. "I'm correct in

139

calling myself your future mother-in-law, am I not, Will?''

This time his eyes held. ''You look like my old headmaster asking me, 'You *were* smoking in your room, weren't you, Tobin?' ''

''That doesn't answer my question. Stacy said that one of your reasons for not agreeing to an earlier wedding was that I was planning a big reception and would be disappointed. I've already had a coming-out party and an engagement party. I won't be disappointed.''

Examining a colorless sketch on the wall, Will said, ''Forgive me if I sound—uh—impertinent, Mrs. Hubert, but this is something that concerns only Stacy and me. I can't discuss it with you.''

''Well, then, discuss it with Stacy. But I understand you told her you're going to be all tied up for a time. You can't carry on discussions telepathically.''

''Did Stacy ask you to speak to me?''

Angela didn't dignify the question with an answer and Will turned pink. ''Well, remember you're the one who started this, Mrs. Hubert. Anyway, I can't reach Stacy. She's been very peculiar lately—irritable, moody, jumpy—and she won't tell me what's wrong. People shouldn't marry one another if they don't trust one another.''

Softly Angela said, ''That's the first time I heard *that* part, Will. About people 'shouldn't marry one another.' Does that mean you two aren't getting married at all? Even in the spring?''

''I didn't say that. I said Stacy doesn't trust me.''

''And consequently you're not getting married.''

''That's up to Stacy.''

''*What's* up to Stacy?''

''To show that she trusts me.''

''And how does she do that?''

''By telling me what's bothering her.''

''And then you'll marry her.''

140

"You sound like a lawyer."

"You sound like you're hedging."

"It depends upon what she tells me."

Gently Angela began tapping the table. A minute ticked by before she said, "Maybe she doesn't trust you, Will, because you've shown yourself—untrustworthy. She has no faith in your loyalty."

"Do you know what they're saying around town, Mrs. Hubert?"

"Do you believe them, Will?"

She had caught him off balance. He had expected her to ask what "they" were saying and her counter question upset him. Lighting a cigarette, he looked for an ashtray. Angela pushed a Sèvres dish at him.

"A doctor is in a vulnerable position," he said finally.

"What's more important to you, Will? Your 'position' or—"

She was interrupted by a knock and Gwen saying, "Mrs. Hubert?"

Impatiently Angela went to the door and unlocked it. "Yes?"

"You have visitors."

"Who, Gwen?"

"Mrs. Fruth and Mrs. Gaillord."

Frowning, Angela said, "Please don't leave yet, Will. I'll be right back."

She went out before he could object. Like a caged animal, he paced back and forth, biting and chewing on something invisible. He was alone for only a moment, however, because Caroline came in. She had changed from her school uniform to her home uniform—torn jeans and a paint-streaked shirt. "Hi. Long time no see."

He scowled morosely at her.

"You seem delighted to have my company."

"Can't you dress decently?"

Hurt, she looked down at herself. "*Everybody* dresses this

way. Did you and Stacy have a lovers' quarrel?"

"What a family of busybodies. Where's Jelly Bean? Maybe he'd like to ask me something too."

"You have terrible manners. Did you know that?"

Again he glanced at his watch. "How would *you* like it if I asked *you* personal questions—"

"Ask me. See if *I* care."

"Are you still getting D's in Latin and A's in Lunch?"

"I hope *I* don't have to marry a smart aleck."

He looked at her, dropped into a chair and stubbed out his cigarette. "You won't be marrying anyone unless you do something about that complexion."

"Talk about busybodies."

He got up and put on his coat.

"Wait," Caroline said in panic. "Mother told me to entertain you until she got back. If you go, she'll think I'm a bore."

"If she doesn't know it by now, she'll never know it." He went out and Caroline followed.

"Who'll you marry if you don't marry Stacy?" she asked with false casualness.

For the first time since he had entered the house, he grinned. "You," he said. "That is, if you give up candy."

She turned a bright pink. "I'm not sure I'll accept you."

The door opened below and Stacy came in.

"You'd better be careful," Caroline said quickly, knowing she was about to lose his attention. "If you don't marry Stacy, Andy Newhouse will."

"Will!" Stacy called from below. "Where are you?"

"He's up here, Stace," Caroline shouted back. "He just proposed to me."

"I'll be right up." They heard her heels on the entrance hall marble and then the opening and shutting of a door. In a moment she came flying up. "I saw your car—I was so surprised—do you have some time? Can you stay for—"

"Your mother called me," he started stiffly. "She wanted to talk—" and then he stopped, shocked at the change in her face. She looked as though he had struck her.

He glanced downstairs and said, "Let's not stand here."

She led him to the upstairs sitting room and Caroline tried to follow. "Scram," Will said.

"You just asked me to marry you."

"Not now. Later." Firmly he shut the door. Stacy sat down disjointedly, her legs stiff and her arms hanging. He noticed that she had deep circles under her eyes. "You need a doctor," he said feebly.

She hugged herself, rubbing her arms. "Will—do you remember those old movies—not so old, I guess. There was a rash of them several years ago: husbands trying to kill their wives. The climax generally consisted of the husband offering the wife the poisoned drink. The wife would know it was poisoned and then they'd have the big scene—screams, chairs overturning, vases breaking. After about two minutes of that, the best friend would show up and save the girl.

"Well, what I'm getting at is, without sounding sticky about it, do you know what I would have done if I had been the wife? I would have drunk the poison. If my husband had wanted me to take it, I would have taken it. I mean, that's what I'd do for *you*, Will. Drink the poison, cut my wrists, hang myself—anything.

"But you—obviously you don't feel that way, do you, Will? You love me, but conditionally. The conditions are that I'm pretty, I'm well-heeled and that I would never do anything, *anything* to bring the slightest embarrassment to you."

She didn't lift her eyes so she didn't see the look of disgust on his face. But when he spoke, she almost jumped. "God, what a silly ass you are. You sound like Caroline. 'I'd drink the poison for you, Will, cut my throat.' Frankly I doubt it. But if you did, I'd have nothing but contempt for you."

He started pacing again. "Life's nothing but a juvenile movie

143

to you, isn't it? Histrionics and noble sacrifice, all tied up with a kiss at the end. This isn't a hypothetical murder. Johnny was killed and his mother was damn near killed. And do you know what people are saying? They're saying that *you* did it. Little dewy-eyed you. Is that what you term 'slightly embarrassing'? Do you know what I'd do if I were sure it was true? I'd walk out. Walk out and never come back. Don't get the idea that I'm some sort of a quixotic hero. I'm not about to get mixed up in a mess like that. What good would it do you if I were? Would it really help if I held your hand while they strapped you in the electric chair? All *I* would get out of it is a nasty shock and a loss of reputation. And that reminds me. I have a patient waiting. She may not be willing to take poison for me, but she *is* willing to shell out four hundred dollars if I deliver her baby.''

She remained where she was long after he left. She kept shivering, but she didn't cry. Her hair straggled around her chin, not quite hiding several dark smudges she had acquired in the MacLeod basement. Suddenly she bent and looked under the couch. Finding nothing there, she examined the closet. She seemed obsessed with the idea that someone had been listening, and she went to the door and peered out. Then, remembering something, she ran down the stairs. At the bottom, she listened again and heard muffled voices coming from the drawing room. She tiptoed across the hall to the cloakroom. Although she had hidden the broken spice cabinet under a pile of junk in the MacLeod basement, she had taken the manilla envelopes. They were on the floor of the closet. Before, excited at the sight of Will's car, she had put them in the handiest spot, but now she realized the danger.

Lifting the stack, she hesitated and then she went to the sitting room. She placed the envelopes on a table and built a quick fire with newspapers and kindling. Without glancing at any of them—not even the names—she crumpled the envelopes and fed them to the fire.

144

She watched it go up the chimney, the sad, ugly record of man's errors, miseries, sins, fears and inhumanities—stupidities and crimes jumbled together indiscriminately, and indiscriminately punished by society.

And all of it had been used by Johnny MacLeod—for what? Money? What had it bought him? Whiskey, custom-made suits, club memberships, a ''friend'' in the city—had it been worth it?

Or had he been out for something more than money? Had he needed the ugly information for its own sake? For the power it gave him over his victims? Had he enjoyed manipulating people, changing their lives and making them suffer? He hadn't the brains or the charm or the drive to control people through politics or business—so perhaps this was his way of doing what others could do in more accepted ways.

And what had happened in his thirty-odd years to make that way of life so necessary? What subtle warping process had turned him into what he was? But of course that was a question the world had been asking since witches and demons had been discredited. There was still no answer to the ugliness and the cruelty and the hatred.

Still shivering, she huddled in front of the fire and fed it envelope after envelope. She could derive no warmth, however, from the flame. The door opened and she whirled quickly. When she saw it was Gwen, she sagged with relief.

''You scared me.''

''What are you doing?''

Turning back to the fire, Stacy said, ''Destroying evil,'' and smiled derisively at herself.

''What? Where's Dr. Tobin?''

''He's gone.''

Something about the way Stacy worded it caught Gwen's attention. ''Gone?''

''Gone. Went. Vamoosed. Scrammed. I mean, he won't come back.''

145

Gwen started to exclaim but repressed it. She walked up behind Stacy's hunched shoulders and put her arm around her. "How can you talk like that? He'll come back."

Stacy didn't answer. The telephone rang and Gwen went back out into the hall. "Hubert residence . . . Just a minute, please . . . Caroline!"

"Is it for me?" Caroline screamed from upstairs. "Who is it?"

"Buzzy."

"Buzzy who?" Caroline quipped and became convulsed at her own humor. Not bothering to answer, Gwen went back to Stacy and shut the door. Stacy hadn't moved. "All engaged people quarrel," Gwen said. "He'll call tomorrow. But if he don't, you call him. It's no disgrace."

Stacy continued to stare into the fire.

"What are you burning? School work?"

In a flat, matter-of-fact voice, Stacy said, "Johnny MacLeod's blackmail file."

"Johnny MacLeod's blackmail—!" Gwen's hand dropped off Stacy's shoulder and, frightened, she looked around. Apparently catching Stacy's obsession about being overheard, she tiptoed to the wall nearest the drawing room and listened, but all she could hear was a faint, faraway murmur. "How— Where did you—"

"I went to the MacLeod house and I found it."

"But where was—How—"

"Oh, she's still at the Ketchums'. I called to make sure. If she had come to the phone I would have said I was calling to find out how she was, but the maid said she was too sick to get up. So I broke in—I wonder what the penalty is for *that?*—and I found the file and I'm burning it. I guess there's an additional penalty for destroying evidence. But they can't do much more to you after they tie you in the chair, can they?" she finished up, more to herself than to Gwen.

Gwen listened to the rambling recital as though it were in a foreign language. Almost without thinking about it, she began helping, crushing the envelopes into burnable balls and throwing them into the fire. Then, noticing that Stacy was shivering and in a throwback to the days when Stacy had had to be protected from colds, she tiptoed out into the hall and came back with a sweater which she put on her shoulders.

They waited until the last envelope was a black outline of its former self, and then, after grinding it into a powder, they went out into the hall. The voices in the drawing room had become louder and they stopped to listen.

Angela was speaking in an odd, strained way. "—headed it for eight years," she was saying.

"All the more reason that you ought to make room for someone else," Mrs. Gaillord answered gently.

"Why now?"

"Angela, you're making it harder. You know the circumstances."

"What circumstances?"

"You don't really want me to be more explicit, do you? It would hurt the hospital drive to have your name at the top."

"I see. It would hurt the drive." There was a long silence and Stacy and Gwen remained where they were, paralyzed. It was the sudden pushing back of a chair that made them realize what they were doing. They scurried back to the study and shut the door quietly. Sitting down, Stacy rested her chin in her hand. She listened to the sounds from the hall—the closet door opening, the snap of a hanger, Mrs. Fruth saying, "We're sorry, Angela, but it isn't up to us."

"You've forgotten your gloves."

Silence. Then the sound of the door opening and closing. Nothing. Not even Angela's footsteps leaving the door.

When Stacy spoke again, the matter-of-factness was gone. There was a new element in her voice which caught Gwen's attention. "It's getting bigger and bigger, isn't it? Every moment. Something has to happen. I mean, it's piling up and becoming more potent and pretty soon, like gases in a closed room, it just has to explode."

XIX

"I can't help it," Buzzy said.

Caroline kept her eyes on the street in front of the movie house and didn't answer.

"Anyway, it's cold out here," he went on. "Let's go inside. We didn't see the end."

"Go right ahead. I'm waiting here."

She saw a car go by, a nondescript dark car, and she thought she glimpsed Mrs. MacLeod beside the driver, another woman, but she wasn't sure. Aside from a flicker of surprise that Mrs. MacLeod had left the Ketchums', she gave it no thought.

"Gee, Carrie," Buzzy was saying, "I can't help it if my mother won't—won't let me go anywhere."

"She's letting you go all right, but you're taking someone else."

He turned crimson. It was true his mother had said he could go to the dance, but not with Caroline Hubert. "I'm not going at all," he said wretchedly. He was awkward and pimply —unattractive to adults but apparently irresistible to his own kind.

"Why? That's what I want to know. Why?"

"Because—because I did something cruddy and I can't go out for a while."

"What did you do?"

"A guy's gotta have *some* privacy."

"You can have all the privacy in the world for all I care. Why don't you go inside and watch the movie?"

"Because my popsy told me never to leave a young lady alone." He grinned but received no answering grin. Silently the two of them watched the empty street. The long-standing custom was for one set of parents to drive the daters to their destination and the other set to take them home. Since Buzzy's father had chauffeured them to the movie, Angela or Frank was due to return them.

Miserable, Caroline waited. Her world was changing in an obscure, unpleasant way. Everything was different: at dancing class she sat around more; she hadn't been asked to Eunice Gaillord's house in two weeks; three or four girls who had never refused before had been unable to accept invitations to her house. Tiredly she shifted her legs. The correct thing to have done, she was sure, was to walk home by herself when Buzzy had told her his news. But her mother would have been worried. Besides, it was dark and cold.

A car drew up at the curb, but it wasn't one she recognized. "Caroline!" a voice called and a gray-haired woman leaned out of the window.

Surprised, Caroline peered into the car. The woman seemed faintly familiar.

"Get in. I'm supposed to take you home."

"What?"

"It's a long story. I'll explain on the way."

Caroline glanced at Buzzy, but he was immersed in a world of his own and didn't seem to be paying any attention. Absently he

150

held the front door open for Caroline and then he slid in beside her.

"Where do you live?" the woman asked Buzzy. He told her and they started up. "Where's my mother?" Caroline asked.

"Let's see now, do I turn here? Yes—oh. Your mother and father had to go out and Stacy had a date and the maid —what's-her-name—Gwen wanted to go someplace—"

"Gwen? Where did she go?"

"I don't know. Do I turn here?"

"Yes. Left. Gwen never goes anywhere."

"Well, she had to go somewhere tonight. Wait, I'll explain the rest later. Where do I go now?"

She seemed too intent on her driving to be disturbed and Caroline was silent. When they reached Buzzy's house he hesitated a moment. "Well, see you, Caroline."

"Goodbye," she said, her voice icy. Reluctantly he shuffled away and Caroline sank back into the cushions. What had she done to deserve this, she wondered miserably. Perhaps it was the hidden surge of hope she had felt when the trouble had developed between Stacy and Will. God was punishing her for wanting Will to herself. Especially when she already had Buzzy. Now she had lost them both.

"Where are we going?" she asked when she noticed that the woman had taken a wrong turn.

"Well, that's what I was explaining. When your mother realized there would be no one at home, she called the Ketchums to ask them to take you to their house, but they were busy too. I happened to be there to pick up Mrs. MacLeod—I'm Mrs. MacLeod's cousin, Mrs. Taylor—and I said I'd take you to my house."

"*Your* house? Why couldn't I stay at the Ketchums' with Valerie?"

"Valerie had a date."

151

"Or—couldn't I go to Eunice's—" She stopped, realizing it was no longer that easy, going to Eunice's. "I know what. Why don't you come to our house and sit with me there?"

"Young lady, I'm not a sitter. I volunteered to do your mother a favor, but I have a lot to attend to at home."

"It's very kind of you. I—I—didn't mean— I can't understand where Gwen went. I'm surprised my mother didn't call Kitty. That's my sister's friend. I mean I once spent the night with her—"

"All I know is that Mrs. MacLeod asked me to pick her up at the Ketchums', and when I got there she told me to take you to my house—"

"But isn't she sick?"

"No, she's better, but not well enough to have you there —she wants to rest."

Caroline felt uneasy. If Buzzy's announcement hadn't upset her, she might have questioned the woman before getting into the car. She didn't like her, but she didn't know why. "I have to go home to get my pajamas," she said firmly.

"I'm sorry, Caroline, I don't have the time. I can lend you something of mine."

Conflicting instructions passed through Caroline's mind: "Never go anywhere with someone you don't know." "Always mind your elders." "Beware of strangers." "Don't contradict a grownup."

She felt abandoned. First Eunice, then Buzzy and now even her own family. Although she had seen Angela only two hours ago, it suddenly felt like ages. She had an irrational desire to bury her head in her mother's lap and pretend she was small again. She wanted to tell her about Buzzy's betrayal and ask her what she could do to make up for her sin. She was close to tears, and in order not to make a fool of herself she began to hum "Kansas City."

XX

Like someone in a forgotten museum contemplating a disturbing painting, Stacy looked through the frame of the window at the moonlit landscape of dying fields, spindly-armed trees and the path disappearing into the hushed woods.

Frozen in the silent limbo, a buck waited at the edge of the clearing, head lifted and one eye turned on Stacy. For a long time he remained motionless, and then, unhurriedly, he turned. Just before he melted into the woods, he looked back almost beckoningly, as though inviting her to join him in the shadowy, haunted picture.

Stacy turned as the door opened behind her. It was her mother. "Why are you standing in the dark?" she asked, the sound dropping like foreign matter into a hidden pool. Stacy still listening to a distant voice, didn't answer at once. But finally she said, "Is Dad back yet?"

"I just heard his car. That's why I came down."

Stacy examined her mother. Freshly washed and combed, she looked as calm as always, apparently undisturbed by the visit of the two women that afternoon. She went out into the hall as the front door slammed and Stacy watched the ensuing tableau: the father returning home as though after a hard day's work; the mother, happy and relaxed, approaching to kiss him; and Gwen, the old family retainer, standing by to take his coat. But there was something wrong with the picture. Nothing was quite the way it seemed.

"Where were you all this time?" Angela asked.

"I told you—I was with the architects—for the town pool."

"But it's so late."

"You know how these things go. The price is up by several thousand—and there were changes." Frank looked drawn and puffy-eyed. Stacy went to kiss him and he put his arm around her and squeezed. "You had more meat on you when you were young," he complained. "Now you're nothing but skin and bones."

"If Frank had his way," Angela said, "we'd all be lumpy balls of fat."

"Just one chubby one. That's all I ever asked for. One chubby one for hugging. Even Caroline is dieting. Where is she, by the way?"

"At a movie."

"With whom?"

"Buzzy."

"Buzzy who?" he asked automatically.

Angela glanced at her watch. "It's almost time for me to pick her up—want to come along?"

"I'm pooped, Ange."

"I'll go," Stacy offered.

"Thank you, dear."

Stacy took a suede jacket from the closet and drove into town. The movie house was emptying as she pulled up at the end of the line of cars. As each car filled up, it drove away, and finally only Stacy was left. Annoyed at Caroline for dallying, she parked and went inside. "My sister hasn't come out yet," she told the

154

man at the door. "May I look inside?"

He motioned her into the lit interior. One glance was enough to show her that it was empty. Frowning, she went out again and looked up and down the street. Then she tried the sweet shop, but Caroline and Buzzy were not among the group of youngsters at the fountain. Finally she went into the telephone booth and called Buzzy's number.

"Mrs. Yeager? This is Stacy Hubert. Did we get our signals mixed?"

"Our signals mixed, Stacy? How?"

"I mean, did you pick up Caroline and Buzzy after the show?"

There was a faint pause. "I don't understand. I took them to the movie and your mother was supposed to take them home—"

"Yes," Stacy interrupted. "That's why I called. I'm at the movie house but they're not here."

"Of course not. Buzzy is home."

Alarm streaked through Stacy. "Buzzy's home? Didn't he take Caroline to the movie?"

"I'm afraid we're speaking at cross-purposes. Buzzy was brought home by— Wait a minute, he's telling me. He said some woman picked them up—"

"Some woman?"

"He said she seemed to know Caroline—"

"What woman?"

"He didn't hear her name. Isn't Caroline home?"

"What? No. That is, maybe we passed one another. I'll check. Thank you." Hastily Stacy hung up, changed a quarter at the counter and dialed her own number. "Gwen? Is Caroline there?"

"Here? Isn't she at the movies?"

"Mrs. Yeager said a woman picked them up and took Buzzy home. Never mind. I'm on my way."

Stacy hung up and raced back to her car. She drove home at

155

breakneck speed, and as she started up the driveway she saw her mother and father framed in the doorway.

"Stacy," Angela called out, "wasn't she there?"

"No. She's not home?"

"That kid," Frank said. "I'll give her the dickens when she gets home. Could they have gone somewhere with a bunch of their friends?"

"No," Stacy said, trying to keep her voice natural. "Didn't Gwen tell you? Mrs. Yeager said a woman took Buzzy home and then, presumably, started for our house."

"How long ago was that?" Angela asked.

"Maybe we'd better get the police." It was Gwen who said it first. She was standing behind them, listening.

Benumbed, they all turned to look at her, as though by putting it into words she had made it worse.

"The police?" Frank said slowly. "She hasn't been missing very long. Wait until I get hold of her—"

"Frank, that won't help. Could she have asked to be taken somewhere else?"

"Why?"

"Oh, you know Caroline. Maybe she decided to visit someone."

"Who?"

"Eunice." Angela went to the telephone and dialed a number. She waited a moment, and then, "Gladys? It's Angela. Is Caroline there?"

"Caroline? Why no, Angela. Whatever made you think—"

"Nothing. She isn't home."

"Isn't home?" A note of anxiety entered Gladys Gaillord's voice. "Where can she—"

"That's what I'm trying to find out. Thank you."

"Wait—Angela? Let me know when you locate her."

"Of course." Angela hung up and stood still a moment, thinking. Then quickly she dialed the Ketchum number. When they told her that Harriet had left, she dialed the MacLeod number. "Harriet? It's Angela. Yes, Angela Hubert. Have you seen Caroline this evening?"

"Me see Caroline? Why should I see Caroline?"

"I don't really know. I simply thought—"

"You mean she's missing?"

"Well—she's not home."

"Why did you call me?"

"I—actually I'm calling everyone. Thank you." She hung up quickly while Harriet was still sputtering.

"I'm calling the police," Frank said.

"Wait." Stacy put her hand over her father's to stop him for a moment. "Maybe she's trying to call *us*. We've been tying up the phone too much."

And then, in answer to what she was saying, the telephone rang. Angela whirled back to the table, knocking over a ceramic ashtray. "Yes?" she said breathlessly into the mouthpiece.

There was a moment's silence and then a muffled voice said, "Let me speak to Stacy Hubert."

Puzzled, Angela handed the telephone to Stacy.

"Whoever it is, get them off quick," Frank instructed.

"Is this Stacy Hubert?" the voice asked. It sounded as though it came from a distance.

"Yes. I'm afraid I'm in a hurry—"

"Listen carefully. You don't know me. I'm doing this because I believe in justice—"

"Who is this? What did you say?"

"Never mind who I am. I have your sister."

At first Stacy couldn't digest the words, and then they almost made her sick. "My sister?" she asked faintly. At the mention of Caroline, Frank wrested the telephone from her, but said nothing.

"Call the police," the voice went on, unaware of a change of listeners, "and admit you killed Johnny MacLeod. I know you

157

did it. I saw you there that night. And remember this. *No tricks*. I don't want you saying afterwards you didn't mean it. *Show them the jewelry*. That will convince them. Any tricks and your sister will die.''

There was a click and the telephone went dead.

XXI

The news announcer gave Caroline's name, age and description, but nothing else. Frank had taken charge, called the police, but hadn't mentioned the telephone call—he had only told them that Caroline was missing.

Healey Mockridge, who had been listening to the radio and reading the evening newspaper at the same time, heard the name Caroline Hubert and dropped the newspaper. His mother and father were out and he was alone. Jumping up, he dialed his own number. It was the first time he had heard Kitty's voice since he had walked out, and he felt himself growing suddenly hot, his underarms sticky and forehead damp. "Kitty," he said abruptly, "did you hear the news?"

It took a moment. Incredulously she asked, "Healey?" Her first hello had sounded dead, but now life came back into her voice.

"Did you hear that Caroline Hubert was kidnaped?"

"Yes." There was no way of telling what she was feeling.

"Well—have you spoken to Stacy? Did you—I mean, have they heard from the kidnapers?"

"She wouldn't come to the telephone. I talked to Gwen, but she didn't know anything. I was just getting dressed to go there."

"Wait for me."

Kitty hung up. "Wait for me," he had said, as though it were the most natural thing in the world. She sat down and her heart began to thud in a sick combination of apprehension and anticipation. She might have been single again, waiting for Healey to call for her. The news about Caroline still hadn't sunk in—she was sure it would all turn out to be a mistake.

Jumping up, she ran to the bedroom and looked at herself. She had been ready for bed when she had heard the local news and she was now half dressed. Her hair was terrible, but she put on powder and lipstick, finished dressing and was leaving her bedroom when the front door slammed open.

He glanced at her as she came into the living room, turned away and threw his coat on the chair as though he had never been away. Not sure of what her attitude ought to be, she watched him as he switched on the radio. "Was there anything else? My car radio isn't working. A kid that age—well, if it's an infant, it can't identify the kidnaper. But Caroline will know who—"

"You mean they might *kill* her?" Kitty asked incredulously, the possibility occurring to her for the first time.

The radio emitted a yeah-yeah song and he kept switching, but each station sounded like the last. There was no news on at the moment. Just then the telephone rang and Healey answered.

"Healey?" Elena Ketchum asked, sounding surprised. "I just—I wanted to ask Kitty if she heard about Caroline Hubert."

"Yes. Is there any more news?"

"No—isn't it awful?"

Restlessly Healey motioned to Kitty. "Yes," he muttered. At Kitty he mouthed the words, "Take it." Then, aloud, "Kitty wants to talk to you."

She took it reluctantly. "Hello, Mrs. Ketchum."

"Isn't it terrible?" Elena prompted.

"Dreadful."

"I've been hearing the oddest rumors. Have you heard anything?"

"Rumors? No, I've been home all day—I mean, since I got back from school."

"Well, I was talking to Mavis Haines—don't tell anyone she said it—but she suggested—maybe she was joking—"

"What did she say?"

"She suggested that it was probably Harriet MacLeod who kidnaped Caroline in order to get Stacy Hubert to confess."

"Confess? Confess what?" Kitty asked stupidly.

"Really, Kitty—I know it's a terrible thing to say about Harriet. And, of course, it couldn't have been Harriet because she was here all day until her cousin picked her up—could it have been her cousin?"

"What are you saying, Mrs. Ketchum? Do *you* think Mrs. MacLeod could have done a thing like that?"

Healey went into the other room and picked up the extension telephone.

"No, dear. I told you she was here all day. But, as I said, I wonder if it could have been her cousin—what's her name? —who kidnaped Caroline—"

"I'm getting all mixed up. First of all, Stacy would never —Besides, what would make Mrs. MacLeod's cousin take a chance like that? Kidnaping is a serious offense."

"That's true. But suppose this cousin were terribly fond of Johnny and willing to go the limit to capture his murderer? No—suppose the cousin knows nothing about the kidnaping or, at least, tells the police she knows nothing about it. She could tell the police that Mrs. MacLeod told her to take Caroline somewhere for some reason as a favor to Angela. Then Harriet could call up with the kidnap threat and the cousin could be completely in the dark."

"But what about the radio—"

"This cousin of Harriet's might not be listening to the radio."

"I can't—I mean, anyway, Stacy could never do a thing like that, so what's the purpose of it all?"

"But I think *Harriet* is convinced Stacy did it."

"Well, suppose Stacy did confess—she could repudiate it afterwards."

"Harriet's no fool. She would insist that Stacy give them some evidence—"

"Mrs. Ketchum, do *you* believe Stacy could ever do a thing like that?"

There was a short silence. Then, "No, Kitty, of course not." Another silence, shorter. "But, don't you think, I mean, wouldn't it be wise not to get mixed up in a mess like that?"

"Like what, Mrs. Ketchum?" It was Healey, on the extension.

"Oh—Healey," Elena said breathlessly, "I didn't know you were still on." She said something they couldn't hear, and then Merrill's voice came on and it was a four-way conversation. "Hello there, boy. Glad to hear everything is patched up."

"What?" Healey asked blankly.

"Now, don't give me that what," Merrill said jovially. "It's a small town. Everybody knows that you and Kitty had a difference about something."

"Does everybody know what it was all about too?"

Merrill's voice was still jovial. "No, boy. Not that. Think we're nosy or something?" He laughed.

"Well—we'd better get on our way," Healey said. "We want to see if there's anything we can do for the Huberts."

Again there was a brief silence and then Merrill said solemnly, "Seriously, Healey, do you think you ought to? I mean, go there?"

Neutrally Healey said, "Why not, Mr. Ketchum?"

"How many times have I told you to call me Merrill? What

162

I'm saying is, isn't it better not to have too much to do with the Huberts right now?''

''You mean, because Caroline was kidnaped?''

''Oh, come off it, Healey. You know what I'm talking about.''

''Is it sinking ships you're talking about, Mr. Ketchum''—he hesitated—''and animals which leave them?''

''Sometimes,'' Merrill said, and the voice was one which had carried him through thirty years of company politics, ''when we stick to a sinking ship we take down more than just ourselves.''

Healey was silent and Merrill went on. ''We take down our wives, for one. And sometimes we take down the company we're working for.''

''Oh, *you* come off it, *Merrill*. I can just see the papers printing, 'Healey Mockridge, a friend of the Huberts who happens to work for Narco—' ''

''It's happened. These things have repercussions everywhere. You know, Healey, 'If a hand stinks, cut it off—' ''

''I heard,'' Elena interrupted, ''that Will Tobin hasn't been near Stacy in weeks. Her own fiancé.'' There was a special note in her voice, not of anger but of warning. It reminded Kitty of a teacher who never said anything when she misbehaved but two weeks later would either send a note to her mother or fail Kitty on a test.

His voice suddenly tired, Healey said, ''I'm sorry, Mr. Ketchum. Stacy's our friend.''

After he had hung up, he stared at the telephone for a moment. Then he joined Kitty in the living room. She took his hand and pulled him down beside her on the couch. He neither encouraged nor rebuffed her. She leaned against him, and then, as though against his will, his arm came around her. ''I think I just lost my job,'' he said.

''Oh, I doubt it.''

''For all practical purposes, I mean. They won't actually fire

163

me, but suddenly it won't be possible to move anywhere—that new job—" Abruptly he changed the subject. "Why didn't you ever tell me?"

She knew what he meant. "I'm not like you. I'm a coward."

Again he switched subjects. "I had a good start at Narco. It means beginning again—right at the bottom."

She traced a pattern on his chest with her index finger.

"And Merrill Ketchum can make things rough. I mean, even in other companies."

She sat up. "If we're going, we'd better go."

He lifted her to her feet and she stood for a moment expecting something, but it didn't come. They put on their coats and went out. In the car she kept turning to watch him and finally he said, "What are you waiting for?"

"You know what I'm waiting for."

He drove silently for a while and then, "All right, I forgive you. You were wrong, but I'm willing to share your bed and board again. Particularly since I may not be earning any money for a while."

"Thank you," she said and leaned against him again. "You were just looking for an excuse to come back, weren't you?"

He shoved her away and they drove the rest of the way in silence. All the lights seemed to be on at the Hubert house. As they got out of the car, they saw Patty Conefrey, the school secretary, leaving.

"Patty," Kitty called, "is there any news?"

"No. Nothing, Kitty."

"How is Mrs. Hubert?"

"Awful. She didn't even know I was there—I'm not even sure you ought to go in."

"Well—just for a minute." They walked in without knocking. Frank was in his shirt sleeves, collar open, trousers rumpled, disheveled in a way Kitty would never have believed possible. His damage, however, appeared to be on the outside,

164

whereas Angela's had erupted from within. Like Lo-Tsen, she seemed to have been pushing age back for years, and then to have succumbed in a few hours. She was shrunken-looking, and had retired to a place far within herself, out of contact with the world. All that remained was a spark of humanity alone in the center of a bright, limitless desert. She showed no awareness of the Mockridges.

In that instant, all of Kitty's preoccupations with her own problems vanished and were replaced by a flock of memories: the weeks she had spent with the Huberts when her own parents had gone on trips; the way she and Stacy had always nagged Frank to take them places; the times when they had been older and had begun to dismiss Frank from the room because, "*Really*, we have things to *discuss*"; the evenings they would sit glued to the telephone waiting for a boy to call, and then, when he did, instruct Gwen to tell him, 'Sorry, they've gone out'; the way they would constantly shoo Caroline when she tried to join them; the time they had run away from her in the woods and left her crying and terrified before they had returned to get her.

Kitty sat down beside Frank and said hesitantly, "Mr. Hubert—I heard something a little while ago. It sounds fantastic, but maybe we can call the police, tell them that Mrs. MacLeod's cousin might—"

He looked up at her blankly as though he couldn't recognize her. Then, making an effort to focus, he said, "Kitty?" He took her hand. "You know—she asked me to help her with her Latin—only yesterday. I didn't have to do much. All I had to do was read one side of the page—she said—what did she call it—the positive—and she would give me the comparative—you know, *bonus, melior*—but I told her I was busy—I said don't bother me. Go away. . . ." He stopped and moved his head vaguely. Then, to Kitty's horror, he was suddenly overcome and he buried his face in his hands and sobbed. He had always

165

been so Olympian to her—strong, big, removed from the child-ish difficulties of herself and Stacy—and now she was non-plussed. The tears streamed down her own face, unheeded, but she could think of nothing to say, nothing to do.

Suddenly, Healey walked out to the hall and she became aware of something which had only touched her peripherally before. Above Frank's sobs, she heard male voices arguing. She recognized one immediately—Dr. Trowbridge, the minister, but the other puzzled her for a moment. Will? No. Then she had it. Andy Newhouse. What was *he* doing here?

"Wait a little while," Andy was saying. "They don't mean it." And Dr. Trowbridge, "Let me talk to Harriet MacLeod first."

At the mention of Harriet MacLeod's name, Kitty remembered again what Elena had said. She jumped to her feet but she was too late. "Give me the police," Stacy was saying. "No, it's not an emergency. . . . This is Stacy Hubert. I'm confessing to the murder of Johnny MacLeod."

XXII

It repeated itself endlessly, a series of pictures thrown on a screen.

First, there was a deserted stretch of road, a place where it curved so that it was impossible to see far in either direction. Both banks were covered with decaying vegetation, spilling over the sides and creeping up on the road itself. The only sounds in the thick atmosphere were the caws of the crows flapping up and down over something. In the strange light every detail of the scene was clear. Her eyes moved in like a camera on a scummy pond and just then, beneath the surface she caught sight of a movement. Something alive was rolling in mucous horror, curling the slime into jelly. Just as the outline was beginning to grow clearer, however, the picture changed.

The scene was the same, but the time had changed. It was as though millions of years had passed. Now the overripe vegetation was gone and everything was dead. In an icy, dry silence, the stalk-like trees were soldiers guarding an already ambushed camp. Even the clouds in the overcast sky were motionless, reflected in the thin ice over the pond.

Then, into this world of nothing, came a creature which should have died out long ago. It shot out from behind the white ash and poplars like an arrow. Shadowy in the dull light, the creature was quivering with terror. It stopped to listen, but no sound came from the picture. Pitifully, head still turned towards the darkness from which it had come, the figure moved closer and closer to the brink of the other, the unknown horror lying in wait.

She tried to scream a warning, but her voice couldn't carry to that time and place. The creature was drawn closer and closer to the muck, and suddenly one of its feet slid from under it. Clutching fiercely at the air, it fought to regain solid earth, a silent scream of torment contorting its face. The more it struggled, the faster it was sucked downwards, and as she watched in agony, its head went under. In that last moment she caught sight of the features. The face belonged to someone she loved.

Caroline woke up, the sound of a wail still in her ears. Her eyes were open, but she couldn't move. Her heart thudded sickeningly and she wondered what had happened. Had she screamed aloud or was it part of the—

The dream. That was it. Just a dream. Shutting her eyes, she waited for the ugliness to drain off, like pus from a wound.

It took a long time. Where was her mother? She wanted her mother to tell her everything was all right. Lifting her head, she found the room spinning, and she sank back on the pillow. What was wrong? She felt terrible.

Her room had never been this black. She could always see the night sky through her large windows. A new terror began. Feeling her eyes, she found that they were not covered with anything. She simply couldn't see. She had to find a light. She had to find her mother.

She fought the dizziness and got out of bed, almost sinking to her knees. Then she felt along the wall, trying to find something familiar. Fighting down an impulse to start running like a rat in a maze, she tried to think, but her thought processes were hazy. Perhaps she had been in an accident and had lost her eyesight. Or something had happened to the country and she was imprisoned in a dungeon like the Count of Monte Cristo. Or she had become insane like old Mrs. What's-her-name and was in an institution—perhaps she had been here for years and was an old woman. In any case, she was doomed to remain in the dark forever, never knowing if it was night or day, ignorant of the passage of time, unaware of what was happening in the world.

The thudding in her chest started up again and she felt sick. Where could she go if she had to throw up?

Fighting the dizziness, she continued feeling along the wall. Now and then she stopped to rest her head. There were lights dancing in front of her eyes. Subconsciously she knew she mustn't call out, but she began to cry helplessly. She couldn't remember when she had felt so awful.

Just then her fingers encountered a crack in the wall and she knew she had found a door. She passed her hand over the smooth surface until she located a knob and the door swung open.

The hall, or whatever it was, was as dark as the room had been. She fought down her panic and made herself walk slowly. Still holding on to the wall, she felt her way along a carpeted surface. Suddenly the floor fell away and her arms windmilled backwards. Forcing herself not to cry out, she regained her balance and steadied herself.

Then, carefully, she found the railing and started down the steps. She reminded herself of stories she had read of people who died of fear when only a short distance from safety. "Mummy," she moaned softly, "Mummy," but she continued descending. Finally she saw a gleam of light.

She was so grateful she nearly sobbed aloud. At last she remembered where she was.

She and Mrs. Taylor had driven on a strange highway to an unknown town, past unfamiliar houses to Mrs. Taylor's home—a small two-story structure exactly like all the others on the street. They had had a snack—hot chocolate and cookies —and afterwards she had been unaccountably sleepy. She had hardly been able to stand and Mrs. Taylor had led her upstairs, shown her the bed, and after that she remembered nothing. If the dream hadn't been so terrible, she would probably have slept through the night.

She looked down at herself and saw she was still wearing the skirt, blouse and sweater which she had worn to the movies with Buzzy about a hundred years ago.

"Mrs. Taylor?" she said softly, but she didn't really want her. Something about the woman had inexplicably upset her. She hadn't been mean, but—well, she spoke very little and she stared a lot. When they had first come into the house, Caroline had asked if she could use the telephone, but Mrs. Taylor had talked her into having a snack first. And then she had been too sleepy.

The telephone. Surely someone would be home by now. She wasn't sure how one dialed from here, but she would ask the operator. She started to lift the telephone, but then she heard a door creak upstairs. There was a moment's silence and then a voice asked, "Is someone there? Who's there?"

Some instinct warned Caroline that Mrs. Taylor would never let her call home, and she looked around wildly. Panicky again, she ran towards the back of the house and found herself in the kitchen. The door was locked on the inside and she turned the key and let herself out. For a moment she stood still, shivering. She didn't have a coat. Then, afraid to wait, she went down two steps to a small backyard and from there to the next backyard. She walked quickly through the strange gardens, wondering if Mrs. Taylor would raise an alarm. A dog began to bark and she was terrified of being attacked by some strange animal. Running down an alleyway, she found herself on the street again. She turned a corner, crossed the street and went up another block, trying to make as many twists as possible.

When she felt she was safe for the moment, she stopped to consider her next move. She knew nothing about where she was except that it was about half an hour's drive from Highlands.

Suppose she knocked on the door of one of the houses and asked to use the telephone? But it was awfully late. Most of the houses were dark. How would they react to the sight of a girl on the step asking to use the telephone? Or what if they were friends of Mrs. Taylor's? They might simply drive her back there. Mrs. Taylor would smile and call her hysterical—and after all, wasn't she? Mrs. Taylor hadn't hurt her. She was doing Mummy a favor. That's all.

But nevertheless, she didn't want to go back. She disliked Mrs. Taylor, she disliked the house, she disliked the dizzy feeling she had had upon awakening and, maybe without reason, she was afraid.

Then don't mention Mrs. Taylor. Simply make up a story. But, if by some accident, she *did* pick the house of a friend of Mrs. Taylor, the people might know who she was anyway. The thing to do was to find a policeman. If you're ever lost, Mummy said, don't go to anyone except a policeman.

Miserably cold, she wondered how to find a policeman. She had never felt so helpless and deserted in her life. Never before had she been without someone she knew and trusted. What was happening back at Mrs. Taylor's house? Was *she* calling the police? What was happening at home? If she went to the police, would *they* take her back to Mrs. Taylor? "Mummy," she moaned again.

How did one find a police station? Always walk downhill when you're lost, Stacy once said. Downhill was generally where the river was or the railroad station or the stores—the center of town. She began walking downhill, taking any turn

171

that looked lower than the last. But instead of the center of town, she found a highway. She was on a broad route that seemed familiar. Perplexed, she wondered what to do next. There was no sign of the town anywhere. Despairing, about to begin crying again, she heard a car approaching from the right. She shrank back. If there was one rule Angela had impressed upon her it was that one didn't accept rides from strangers. The car slowed down and a woman called out, "Are you in trouble?"

XXIII

They all sat up straighter when they heard the police siren—like people expecting company. Everyone except Angela turned to watch the door. As though she were a hostess, Stacy got up first and then had to reach out to steady herself. She grabbed a lamp, which tottered and would have fallen if Healey hadn't caught it.

Frank opened the door to two men wearing ordinary business suits. As they entered, another car drew up with two uniformed policemen in it.

"That confession—" Frank was saying. "It doesn't mean anything. My daughter made it because we received an anonymous telephone call—"

"Wait a minute," one of the men said. He was large, a little past middle age and he looked kindly. "Who are *you?*"

"I'm Mr. Hubert. My daughter—"

"Your daughter was the one who made the telephone call to the police?"

"Yes. The reason—"

"Could we talk to her?"

"Here I am," Stacy said. She walked steadily now and her voice was normal.

"Listen to me," Frank went on desperately. "This crackpot—"

"Now wait a minute, Mr. Hubert. One at a time."

"Dad," Stacy said, her voice dead. She put her hand on his arm and tightened her fingers.

"You're the one who confessed to killing John MacLeod?" the detective said to Stacy.

"Dammit," Frank shouted, flinging off Stacy's hand. "Listen to me. She did it because a crackpot telephoned us and said they'd kill Caroline if she didn't confess. Where *is* Caroline? Why aren't you out looking for her instead of bothering us?"

"I think I know where Caroline may be," Kitty said, but no one heard her.

To Stacy, the detective said, "Is what your father said the truth? Did someone call and say they'd kill the kid if you didn't confess?"

"Well—yes—but I killed him."

"It's ridiculous," said Dr. Trowbridge. "I've known Stacy Hubert all her life—"

"Who are *you*?" the detective asked, getting annoyed.

"I'm Peter Trowbridge. I'm the minister at Highlands Protestant Episcopal Church and I—"

"Oh yes. Sorry, sir."

"This girl is confessing to something she didn't do in order to save her sister."

"I bet Harriet MacLeod has Caroline," Kitty said.

"Now who the hell are *you*?" the detective snapped, losing control.

"I'm Kitty Mockridge. It's only a theory but I bet—"

"God—a theory—"

"Harriet took Caroline in order to get Stacy to confess."

"Mrs. MacLeod is home," the detective said.

"Well, then her cousin took Caroline. Why don't you make Mrs. MacLeod tell you where her cousin lives—"

174

"Do you know what you're all doing?" Stacy said, her voice rising hysterically. "You're killing Caroline. They'll kill her. I *did* murder Johnny MacLeod, and I can prove it. I know where the jewelry is."

It was as though a fuse had blown and the current animating all the figures in the hall had died, leaving them frozen into position. Kitty, who had started towards Stacy as if she intended stopping her mouth with her hand, hardened in her tracks; Healey remained poised in the process of lighting a cigarette; Frank had lifted his hands to his eyes to rub them, and he remained locked that way; Dr. Trowbridge was congealed into an attitude of disbelief; Angela still hadn't moved; and Andy Newhouse simply shut his eyes.

Then suddenly the detective who was second in command lifted his hand for a silence he already had and said, "What's that?"

It was unexpected and they all stared at him stupidly. "I hear—like a humming—wait—do you smell—"

Docilely they cocked their heads and sniffed, as though they had nothing more important on their minds.

Healey moved first. "Gas," he snapped, and the word released them. Healey in the van, they stampeded towards the kitchen. "We don't have gas," Frank panted. "The whole house is electrified."

One of the detectives remained close to Stacy as they all crowded into the kitchen. He suspected a trick and he reached out to take her arm, but suddenly she ran to the outer door—the one which led to the garage—and tore it open.

She staggered back as the kitchen filled with gasoline fumes.

XXIV

Slowly Caroline stepped out on the road. The couple in the car looked like the kind of people she knew best—middle-aged, well dressed, respectable. With sudden resolve she approached the car and said, "I need a ride to Highlands," although she had no idea whether or not they were headed in the right direction.

The woman examined her doubtfully. "We're passing near there, although we're not going into the town itself. What are you doing—aren't you cold?"

"Yes—uh. Well, you see," Caroline went on, improvising wildly, "I went out with some friends earlier this evening and the boys got fresh—you know. And I told them to stop the car and I just got out and I said I wouldn't ride with them if they acted like that—and they—they just left me." She finished on an interrogative note, almost as though asking them if it sounded logical.

The man and the woman exchanged glances and then the woman said, "Well—we can't just leave her here." He muttered something about getting into trouble, and at that Caroline's confidence in them increased. If they were reluctant about giving her a ride, they must be all right.

"If you could just drop me off at the nearest place to Highlands, I could call home or get a taxi or something. I mean, if my mother is still out—she was going out this evening—I could get a cab to take me home. Maybe you could drop me at a drugstore or something where I could call."

The man looked around helplessly, almost as though expecting her accomplices to jump them any minute. "All right, young lady," he said irritably. "Hop in."

Caroline slid into the back seat and said gratefully, "Oh, it's so nice and warm in here."

"You poor thing," the woman said. "Turn up the heat, Frank."

"Frank! That's my father's name." Caroline felt that the coincidence confirmed her good judgment. "How close will you be passing to Highlands?"

"Well, we have to go through Ralston—"

"Ralston! That's great. Honestly. It's the next town. It's maybe—ten or fifteen minutes from my house. I'll call home. Probably Gwen or Stacy will be home by now—"

"Who are Gwen or Stacy?"

"Stacy's my sister and Gwen's our housekeeper."

"We've been driving all day. We're trying to get to our son's school tonight, that is, the motel near it, otherwise we'd be glad to take you home."

"Please don't worry about it. Ralston is fine. Really."

The woman continued to ask Caroline questions, and apparently she came to the same conclusion that Caroline had reached about herself—this teenager was the kind she knew best. She became more and more reluctant about leaving her.

Suddenly Caroline became aware of familiar landmarks—a four-way intersection, a shopping center, the bank. Happiness overcame her, as though she'd been away for years. "There's the drugstore. You can let me out here."

177

Hesitantly the woman said, "Frank, do you think—"

"Helen, I can't drive much longer—"

"The drugstore is open," Caroline said reassuringly. "See?"

"I hate to leave you. Do you have money for a call?" the woman asked.

"Oh." Embarrassed, Caroline fished in her pockets.

"Here—wait." The woman took out all her change, some dimes, quarters and nickels. "Take this, just in case—and how about the cab?"

"Oh no. Really. Whoever is home will pay for the cab. Anyway, we know them. They'd trust me. Just a dime, please."

"Well, you might lose it." The woman pressed all the change into Caroline's hand and Caroline said, "Thank you —wait—I'd like your name and address so I can send back—" The man started up the engine and the woman turned to wave goodbye.

Caroline, considerably cheered, went into the drugstore, nodded to the man behind the counter and bumped into two boys getting off stools in front of the fountain.

"Caroline!" one of the boys exclaimed as though he'd seen a ghost. "Caroline Hubert!"

Caroline blinked. It was Nicky Meese, the older brother of one of her schoolmates. Imagine Nicky Meese recognizing her, much less speaking to her.

"Hi there," she said offhandedly.

"Where've you been?"

"What?"

"You've been kidnaped—I mean, weren't you?"

"Kidnaped!" Astonished, Caroline repeated, "Kidnaped! Me?" And then all her suspicions about Mrs. Taylor flowed back. Why was she so surprised? Hadn't she felt all along that there was something wrong with the woman? And hadn't she run away? She'd been right after all. "Boy, wait'll I tell Eunice.

Say, Nicky, can you take me home? I was just going to call
—maybe you can drive—''

''Sure, come on. Let's go.'' The boys dragged her to a new
car standing at the curb and hustled her in. All three began
talking at once. Caroline was so excited she was nearly incoher-
ent, and not the least of her excitement stemmed from the fact
that Nicky Meese was driving her home.

''What happened? Tell us about it,'' the other boy said.

''Well—Mrs. Taylor, Mrs. MacLeod's cousin, picked me up
at the movies—''

''What do you mean? Weren't you kidnaped?''

''Well—gosh, I don't know.'' Deflated, she said, ''*You're*
the one who said I was.''

''It was on the radio. Your father got a call—''

''Then I *was* kidnaped.''

''Why would Mrs. MacLeod's cousin kidnap you?''

''I don't know.''

''Maybe it wasn't Mrs. MacLeod's cousin. Maybe she only
said she was.''

''I never thought of that!'' Caroline exclaimed.

''What did she look like?''

''Well, she was gray-haired. Thin. Kind of, come to think of
it, she *looked* like Mrs. MacLeod.''

''That's funny. But how did you get away? What were you
doing in Ralston?''

''Well, I went to Mrs. Taylor's house and I went to sleep. But
I woke up and I felt funny—do you think I was drugged?''

''How should *I* know? Go on.''

''And I escaped from the house and I hitched a ride to
Ralston.'' As she told it, she began to feel that she had done
something extremely brave and resourceful.

''Why did you escape from the house? What made you
suspicious?''

''I don't know. She just wasn't—I didn't like her, that's all.''

"I met Mrs. Taylor once," Nicky said. "She didn't look like a kidnaper to me."

"Well, I don't know. She said my folks were all away and that Mrs. MacLeod told her to take me to her house—Mrs. Taylor's."

"Maybe Mrs. MacLeod kidnaped you, not her cousin. I mean, she could have fooled her cousin and said your mother wanted you to go there—"

"Why would Mrs. MacLeod want to kidnap me?"

He shrugged and said again, "How should I know?"

They were turning up the road that led to the house now. "Maybe she thought she'd get even—" He stopped talking and exchanged glances with the other boy.

"What're you looking like that for?" Caroline asked.

"Nothing. Anyway, I don't think Mrs. Taylor knew about the kidnaping. She'd get into trouble for that. Mrs. MacLeod wouldn't care about trouble—she'd do anything for Johnny."

"What has Johnny got to do with it?"

"Say, there's a police car in front of your house."

Excited again, they all tumbled out and ran towards the house.

"Mummy, Daddy," Caroline shrieked. "I'm here."

The house was all lit up, but there didn't seem to be anyone around. They dashed through, shouting, and again Caroline felt afraid, as though she'd been away for years and something terrible had happened.

Just then Andy Newhouse and Dr. Trowbridge appeared. Both of them looked odd. At the sight of her, however, their expressions lightened. "Caroline!" Andy Newhouse said, and although he hardly knew her he picked her up and hugged her. Surprised, she stared at him. Fleetingly she wondered if she could marry him instead of Will.

"Where's my mother?" she asked. "Where's everybody?"

"Something's happened. Maybe you oughtn't—"

Remembering her dream, she pushed him out of the way and ran to the back of the house. She could hear sounds coming from there. She was so frightened, she could hardly breathe. She burst into the kitchen and then she stopped.

She saw a man with a towel over his face coming out of the garage, and then she noticed that though it was cold, all the windows were open. Just then Stacy came out of the garage with Kitty and Kitty acted as if Stacy were sick. She put Stacy on a chair and covered her shoulders with her own coat. Stacy was shivering and her lips were blue—and no wonder, with all the windows open.

Then two men came out of the garage carrying something. There was no place else to put it so they put it on the floor. Stacy took off Kitty's coat and covered the form stretched out at their feet, but not before Caroline had caught sight of Gwen's face.

She lay there in that familiar room where she would never chat with Stacy again, never wash a cut of Caroline's again, never discuss a grocery list with Angela again, never fix a breakfast for Frank again—looking as though she were asleep, her chin on her shoulder, her arm across her chest, and on her face the peaceful expression of someone who has done well.

XXV

The trees which Angela had planted everytime one of the girls had a birthday had taken over the entire entrance, overlapping one another, and crowding out the sun. Frank's expensive lawn was covered with crab grass and dandelions, and the once-black driveway was now a dusty gray. Buried in the tangle of rhododendron, ivy and yews, the house itself was faded and peeling. Splinters of wood had been stripped off the front door, leaving raw, dirtied wounds. Angela's flower beds were choked with weeds, and only an occasional phlox had survived the ruin. On one side of the Hubert property the farm had been sold to a large family, and on the other side a new house was going up. The silence which had once been broken by an occasional cowbell was now splintered by children's voices.

"I had no idea," she kept repeating. "How could nine years make such a difference? I just had no idea."

"I guess that's why they always visited us. They didn't want us to see it."

The two of them got out of the car and rang the bell while still examining the decay. She lifted her eyes so that the stinging tears wouldn't spill over, as though the saddest part of the visit was the fact that the garden was neglected or the house unpainted. A fly buzzed on the screened window, and far down the road they heard the hum of traffic.

Frank stood blinking in the sunlight, staring at them as though he hardly knew them. He rubbed his eyes, shaded them, and finally exclaimed, "Stacy—baby—" as she threw herself into his arms.

Inside it was worse. Almost no light penetrated the dusty windows. The draperies were all the same, but they hung limply and smelled of dust. When her eyes became adjusted to the gloom, she could see the worn, soiled spots on the couch, the cigarette hole in the Persian rug, and the threadbare pathway, like a trail through the woods. But most of all, the air of decay emanated not from age or neglect, but from a corrosion of a different sort, a rot which had been gnawing away at the anatomy of the house since the beginning.

"Why didn't you call us in time?" Stacy said finally. "I should have been here."

"She hated funerals. You know. She didn't want you or Caroline to have to go to hers."

"Where are Caroline and Nicky?"

"They didn't know when you'd arrive—they're at Kitty's. We're all invited there later. . . ." His voice had acquired an odd habit of dying out rather than coming to a halt.

Stacy sank into the couch and shut her eyes tentatively, as though to see what would happen—and what happened was that nine years were erased and the French doors were open to the fragrance of freshly cut grass, and her mother was wearing the long gray chiffon dress again, and Caroline was saying, "Are you kidding? It's your engagement party." She had been so happy that day, the day of her engagement to Will, or at least in the beginning she had. But certainly the cancer had been present. She had felt it later on in the screech of the cicada, in the

183

way Joseph Ritacco had said, "Hubert? Haven't we met before?" in Kitty's light mocking voice telling her, "Darling, all over the world insects are eating one another. Why, in some places, even men—", in the shocked tones of the woman saying, "Jim Hostetter committed suicide this afternoon."

"You know," she said abruptly, "Will came back after —after Gwen died. He asked me to marry him."

Andy looked at her oddly, but her father seemed to follow her train of thought. "They all came back after Gwen died," Frank assented, nodding his head. "Every last one of them. When it didn't matter. Elena and Merrill and the Pattersons and the Gaillords—every last goddamned one of them. Apologetic as hell. After all, it was only Gwen who had killed Johnny. Only the maid. Who cared what her nasty little secret was?"

As though Frank hadn't spoken, Stacy went on. "He told me how fond he had been of Gwen. He reminded me—as though I needed reminding—of things she'd done, funny little mistakes in her speech. . . ." Stacy stared at the ceiling. "I wonder why I'm talking about Gwen. It's Mummy who just died."

"Take it easy, Stace," Andy said. He began walking up and down, watching her uneasily. He knew the signs.

"It's funny," Stacy went on. "I'd been so crazy about him. I'd have done anything for him. Then, when he came back, I felt nothing. I couldn't wait to get him out of the house. It wasn't that I hated him. It was just that—the sight of his face, the sound of his voice—it made me sick." She began to trace a pattern on the rug with the toe of her shoe, and then she flung back her hair in the old gesture, but it was no longer shoulder length and didn't fly back. She hadn't changed in weight, and only a few tiny lines around her eyes showed the passage of time. Will had been right—look at the mother.

Andy, walking from shelf to shelf, found a book and opened it at random. He stared at the inscription for a moment, hesitated and then decided not to show it to Stacy. "I think—I'd like to

184

give this to Caroline,'' he said. ''She might want it for little Carrie.''

Stacy got up and reached for the book. Reluctantly he handed it to her. It was *Wuthering Heights*, and on the flyleaf Angela had written, ''To Caroline—for cracking eighty. Not in golf, but in English. Mother.''

Stacy kept reading the inscription as though it were very long, and then she undid a button on her cotton dress and ran a finger around her hot neck. When she sat down Andy put his arm out, pulling her close, and automatically she adjusted to the curve of his body. ''I wonder if it's possible for a person to die because she had nothing to live for.''

''She had something to live for, Stacy—little Carrie—our kids—it was just a heart attack.''

''But her heart was good.''

''It happens.''

She took Andy's hand and held it between her own two and then lifted it to rub across her cheek. ''Dad, you'll have to come back with us now.''

Frank didn't hear her at first. He continued sitting opposite them, watching the dusty window. Then he lifted his eyes. ''No.''

''Why not? You can't just—''

''We stayed on before. I can stay now.''

''But not alone. The house is so big.''

''With Andy in the army, you keep moving. I'm too old to move.''

''I can't understand how you can stay. They were so hateful, so full of pestilence—''

''There's pestilence everywhere,'' Andy said, the ghost of a self-mocking grin on his face. Frank glanced at him and then away. He nodded automatically, his head bobbing like a doll's. ''I'm tired of running.''

''Running?'' Stacy frowned.

Again Frank glanced at Andy, and this time the look held. Outdoors a child shouted, "But if you did, you wouldn't and we can't," but inside, everything was hushed. Even the flies had stopped buzzing. Finally Frank got to his feet. For the first time she noticed that he had gained weight, but not from overeating. His muscles were slack, evidently he had given up the golf, the swimming, the town activities. Without explaining, he walked out, moving like an old man.

It took a long time. They both listened, tracing his progress, and after what seemed like hours, they heard his footsteps descending the stairs again. Finally he stood in the doorway, holding an envelope.

Without thinking, Stacy shrank back. She recognized her mother's cream-colored stationery.

"Take it," Frank said. "She left it for you."

Stacy couldn't move. She could see it had actually been sealed with wax—which was like Angela. She was afraid she would choke. She hadn't cried when she had received the telegram. She hadn't cried when they had made their arrangements and left the children. But now, suddenly, the great gasping sobs gagged her. "I can't—it's like—like a voice from the grave—"

Her control broke, the tearing spasms almost ripping her apart. Andy, who had seen it coming, shut his eyes and waited, but Frank got up and left the room. The whole house seemed filled with her sobs, as though upon her shoulders had fallen the task of filling some strange vacuum. He held her tightly but didn't try to stop her. Years of restraint poured out on the front of his shirt, soaking through to his skin, but he didn't move. Almost remotely he listened to the floor boards creaking above his head and the children outside and the robin in the Japanese cherry tree.

Finally, when her body stopped shuddering, Andy reached into his pocket and handed her his handkerchief. "You don't

186

have to read it if you don't want to, Stace," he told her.

She blew her nose, dried her eyes and took the letter. On the back, Angela had written in a business-like way, "For Stacy —when I die."

She stared at the sentence for a long time, and then carefully she broke the seal. There were five monogrammed sheets inside, all filled with Angela's neat handwriting.

"My darling," it began.

"When you read this, I'll be dead. Was it cowardly of me not to tell you before? I don't know. I don't know why I'm telling you now—except that I feel sure you've always suspected. And I want you to have the whole story. Also, I want you to know what Gwen did for us.

"I should have acted sooner when Harriet called that night in her disguised voice and said she had kidnaped Caroline. But I must have gone into shock. I considered Harriet capable of anything. Of course I didn't know until afterwards that the cousin had Caroline and had only agreed to take her on condition that nothing happened to Caroline and that Harriet take the blame.

"Afterwards it was too late for me to help Gwen. If I had told the truth, her sacrifice would have been for nothing.

"I think you guessed almost immediately that it was I who killed Johnny. You probably either saw me as I went out or when I came in and when you heard the news the next day, you knew who had done it. And Gwen? Did she think it was *you?* I had on that old polo coat and a scarf—maybe she saw me too. But I don't know if she would have done it for me. But she would have done anything for you. And, of course, she did.

187

"There are some things I don't think you suspect even now. Gwen was my sister. When we first decided on our course of action, we wanted to take Gwen, but we knew she would never fit in. She finished the eighth grade and went straight into domestic service.

"She never had what I did—ambition, drive, whatever it was. I finished high school, and then, with Gwen's help, was graduated from college, too. Why did I let her work to put me through? It was our only chance. And I worked, too—I took any odd jobs I could to help pay my way through.

"I was a librarian when I met your father. That was the strangest part of it. Meeting Frank in a library. You see, he too had ambition and drive. But he already had the money. Now he wanted the education.

"How did he get the money? That's the part you will probably never be able to understand. You've always had everything—and we never had anything. Do you remember those houses we passed in New York City that summer day and you saw the dirty children playing in the hot streets? You said you'd rather die than live like that.

"Well, *we* lived like that when we were young. Your father and I. And we felt as you did—we'd rather die. But we found another way. Or your father did. With him, it started with adolescent gangs and adolescent crimes. And it didn't stop there. It got bigger and bigger. I never knew the details. I didn't want to know them. But I didn't mind spending the money.

"You've read about 'crime syndicates.' The words probably conjure pictures of 'molls' and gun-toting gangsters—it

188

wouldn't have occurred to you that the members of the syndicates could be 'nice' people like your mother and father, with nice children, like you and Caroline.

"Someone was killed. Your father and a few others were implicated. They got a good lawyer. Only one received a stiff sentence; the others, including your father, went to jail for only a short time and were paroled. That's what Johnny found out. That and the fact that no one ever leaves the syndicate. To this day your father is a member.

"You were born after your father was paroled.

"I wish—well, you have Dede now and you can guess what I would feel whenever I would watch you sleeping at night. Or look into your eyes when you sat on my lap. I had to protect you. And that's when we decided to fabricate a new life.

"We invented a new name and a new background. I can't go into the details. It wasn't easy. Gwen wanted to come—we had no other family—it was she who suggested she come as our maid. We couldn't take a chance on any strange live-in help anyway, but we tried to make it as easy on her as possible. And I don't think she ever really minded. She had you and Caroline.

"It went very well—even the best club in the county accepted us without question. We were good at it. And then came the engagement party and Joseph Ritacco.

"He was no blackmailer. Only a newspaperman who was curious. I think he was sorry about it afterwards. But I guess our snobbishness annoyed him and he mentioned it to Johnny—and that was all Johnny needed.

"Johnny was an expert. He was always alert, and once given the scent he could snoop out anything. Of course he wouldn't have been so successful if he hadn't had cooperation—from all the 'nice' people. The people who listened and repeated.

"Anyway, I knew that even if we paid, there would be no end to it. It would go on as long as Johnny lived. And I had gone through too much to give it up. Don't think I did it for you and Caroline alone. I did it for myself.

"I had no compunction about killing Johnny. (If you play a dirty game, you don't use clean rules.) Or about trying to kill Harriet. I feel sure she always knew what Johnny was up to, but like me she didn't mind spending the money.

"Please try to be happy, darling. Make the most of what Gwen gave you. Don't tell Caroline—she never suspected anything. Destroy the letter and go back home. I never did believe the one about 'the sins of the fathers . . .' "